Carrot Top

Eight lively stories about Melinda, her family and friends, living together and playing together, sometimes fighting with each other, always living life to the full.

Other Young Lions Storybooks

Stories by

NIGEL GRAY

Carrot Top

Illustrated by Robin Bell Corfield

Young Lions
An Imprint of HarperCollinsPublishers

For Gina

First published in Great Britain by Orchard Books 1987
Published in Young Lions 1989
This impression April 1992

Young Lions is an imprint of
HarperCollins Children's Books,
a division of HarperCollins Publishers Ltd,
77–85 Fulham Palace Road,
Hammersmith, London W6 8JB

Text copyright © Nigel Gray 1987
Illustrations © Robin Bell Corfield 1987
All rights reserved

Printed and bound in Great Britain by
HarperCollins Manufacturing, Glasgow

Contents

— The Workmen —

Melinda was bored. She had nothing to do. She went out to play in the street. Some Indian ladies in lovely saris, mauve, green and gold, went by. They were going to Harry's shop.

Melinda walked up the street, being careful not to tread on the cracks in the pavement. Young Sid was trying to sell a watch to Squint-eyed Jim. Sid pulled up the sleeve of his jacket and he had watches all up his arm. Jim can't see very well. He put his nose on a watch so that he looked as though he was smelling it, like a dog. Sid saw Melinda watching them.

"Clear off!" he snapped.

Aunty Anne came down the street pushing old Mary

in her wheelchair. Melinda's mum called Aunty Anne the street newspaper. "Hello, Melinda," said Aunty Anne. "It's little Melinda," she told old Mary.

"I can see that," Mary said crossly. "I could hardly miss her with *that* hair."

"Has your dad got himself another job yet?" Aunty Anne asked Melinda.

"Yes," Melinda said.

"Where at?" Aunty Anne wanted to know.

"Don't know," said Melinda.

"I'd better pop in and see if your mum wants anything from Harry's," Aunty Anne said. "Out the way!"

Melinda stepped off the pavement to let Aunty Anne go by with the wheelchair. Then she went slowly on her way up the street, bobbing up and down, with one foot in the gutter and the other on the kerb. Soon she became a monorail train. She began to run, balanced on the edge of the kerb, making a monorail train sort of sound. Then Tom started shouting from across the road.

Tom was in Melinda's year at school, but he was in

Miss Pye's class. Melinda was in Mr Domingo's. Tom was standing on a pile of builders' sand.

"Watcher, Carrot Top!" he yelled.

Melinda's monorail train came to a halt.

"Carrot Top! Carrot Top!" Tom leapt off the sand

and bounced up and down in the road. "Carrot Top! Carrot Top!" He danced around like a Red Indian brave.

"You shut up, Tom Tit," Melinda said. Melinda hated people going on about her hair.

Tom pulled a face, then stuck out his tongue. "Carrot Top! Carrot Top!" he chanted.

Then a workman came out of Mr McCarthy's house. Mr McCarthy had died. Some Chinese people had bought the house. They were having it done up before they moved in. Mr McCarthy had been old and had let it go to rack and ruin. Melinda recognised the workman. It was Mr Clack. He lived in the next street, and he had once come to do a job in Melinda's house. Melinda's dad had knocked down the dividing wall between the living-room and the front room, and the ceiling had nearly fallen in. Melinda's mum had sent her running to fetch Mr Clack. She'd had to say it was an emergency.

Mr Clack set his barrow down beside the heap of sand. He rubbed his back and looked up at the sky. He closed his eyes and enjoyed the feel of the sun on his face for a little while. Then he opened his eyes and looked first at Tom and then at Melinda.

"Carrot Top! Carrot Top!" Tom sang.

Mr Clack walked round the sand and squatted near Tom. "Now, what's to do?" he said. "Are you making her cry?"

"Look at her hair," Tom yelled, dancing all around. "It's all sort of ginger — there's something wrong with her head."

Mr Clack laughed. "You cheeky basket." He picked Tom up and swung him up in the air. "Look at your own," he said. "It's all frizzy on top. You'd make a very good mop for cleaning the floor." He tipped Tom over and held him by his heels. Tom was hanging upside down like a bat in a belfry, laughing and laughing. Then the man stood him down the right way up.

Mr Clack went over to Melinda. "Now then, lovely," he said. "No need to cry. Come on. Dry those eyes. Cheer up." He took Melinda's hand. They crossed the road together and sat down in the sand. The man patted a place beside him and Tom came and sat down too.

"What's your favourite colour?" Mr Clack asked.

Tom said, "Blue."

Melinda said, "Green."

"I love the colour of carrots," Mr Clack said. "They're flaming orange — the colour of sunshine. Like your hair." And he ruffled Melinda's hair with his big hand.

"Her hair's ginger," Tom said.

"What else is ginger?" Mr Clack asked.

Tom said, "A ginger biscuit."

"Yum, yum," said the man, licking his lips and rubbing his tummy.

Melinda said. "A ginger cat."

"Prrrr, prrrr," said the man, stroking his pretend whiskers.

Then they heard some chimes, like a giant's music box. Mr Clack shouted, "Paddy! It's ice-cream time."

"OK, Will," another voice answered from inside the house.

Then the ice-cream van came into the street. Mr Clack called, "You'd better get four." And the workman Paddy came out of the house into the sun-

16

shine. Melinda and Tom both sat and stared, because
Paddy had ginger hair.

They ate their ice-creams sitting in the sun on the
heap of sand. "Sure, this is the life," Paddy said, when

his ice-cream was eaten. He lay back with his hands behind his head and stretched his long legs into the road. "This is like being on holiday on a golden beach. It's what I'll do if ever I'm rich."

After that Melinda and Tom played on the sand, getting in the way, until it was the workmen's knocking-off time. The two men came out of Mr McCarthy's house with little canvas bags hanging from their shoulders and their coats over their arms. Paddy locked the door.

Mr Clack said, "Ta, ta, Mop Head. Ta, ta, Carrot Top." And he ruffled their hair.

Paddy put his hand in his pocket and brought out two shining ten pence pieces. He said, "Here's some pennies to spend in the shop."

"Thank you," said Melinda.

"Ta," said Tom.

And together, clutching the coins in their hands, they ran off down the road to see what treats they could find in Harry's.

— The Very Bouncy Ball —

Melinda's mum said, "Melinda, can you go over the shop for me and get a pint of milk. Where's my purse?" Melinda's mum was always losing her purse. She looked on the chairs. Behind the clock. In the bread bin. She looked everywhere. "Have you seen it, Melinda?"

"No, Mum."

Mum found her purse. It was in her apron pocket.

Melinda went to Harry's shop. Aunty Anne was telling Harry about her pains. Aunty Anne was always telling people about her pains. Melinda looked along the sweet counter. And there, among the usual sweets, was a surprise. There, among the liquorice laces and bubble gum and penny chews, was a box of Very Bouncy Balls. They were transparent, with lots of colours swirling inside them. Red and blue and yellow and orange and white. They were like giant rubber marbles.

Aunty Anne took her shopping and went out. "Now then," said Harry. "What can I do you for, little Melinda?"

"How much are them balls?" Melinda wanted to know.

"They're 44p, my love, them," said Harry. "Want one?"

Melinda looked in her pocket. She only had 4p of her own money. "No," she said sadly. "I only want a pint of milk for my mum."

Harry handed her a bottle of milk. "Mind you don't go dropping it," he said. "It won't bounce like them balls will."

Melinda carried the milk home. "Thank you, love," her mum said. "Stick it in the kitchen, will you. The baby's woke up now. I shall have to go and fetch him."

"Mum?"

"What, love?"

"Can I have my pocket money today?" Melinda asked.

"Well, it's only Thursday. You're not due it till Saturday."

"Yes, but there's some Very Bouncy Balls in Harry's shop, and they're 44p, and I've only got 4p left."

"44p for a ball?" said Mum. "But you wouldn't have any spending money left for the rest of the week."

"I know," Melinda said. "But they're ever so lovely."

"All right. Take 40p out of my purse."

"Where's your purse, Mum?"

"I don't know, dear. You'll have to look for it."

Melinda found the purse. It was in the dirty washing. She took 40p and ran to Harry's shop.

"Hello," said Harry. "You back again?"

"Can I have one of them Very Bouncy Balls?"

"Of-course you can, my love," Harry said, picking a ball out of the box.

"No. Not that one," Melinda said.

Harry picked out another.

"No. That one there."

Harry picked out another one.

"That's right."

"They're all the same, my dear," Harry grumbled.

But they weren't. They all had different patterns.

Melinda went out onto the street. She looked at the gorgeous colours winding around each other in her ball, and she smiled to herself. Then she threw the ball down hard onto the road. It bounced up, high, high, as high as the bedroom windows. Then down it came — BANG! right on Jamaica Joe's car. Then across the road and — BANG! again, against Old Mother Hammer's window. Then it began to bounce all over the place. Melinda chased it. The street dogs chased it. Janet's Pip caught it.

"Drop it!" Melinda shouted angrily.

She took her Very Bouncy Ball away from Pip and wiped the wet off on her dress. She turned her lovely ball round in her hands, examining it carefully. There was a tooth mark on it! "You've spoilt it!" she said.

She saw Tom looking at her out of his window. She waved, but he didn't wave back. Then Calvin and Janet and Marzipan came along. (Marzipan's real name was Mahzabeen — but nobody called her that.)

"What you got?" Calvin asked.

"Cor, let's see," said Janet.

"It's smashing," Marzipan said. "Can we play?"

Janet took the ball and threw it down as hard as she could. It bounced high, high, as high as the roofs. Then down it came. It hit the lamppost, knocked on Granny Gray's door, and leapt about all over the road. They all ran after it. Whoever caught it, bounced it, and they all ran after it again. Sometimes one of the dogs caught it.

"They'll spoil it," Melinda complained.

"I know," said Janet. "Let's go down by the tip and play. There's no dogs down there."

"I'm not going there," said Marzipan. "That's right by the witch's house."

"She's not a witch," said Calvin.

"She is," said Marzipan. "My sister said."

"Your sister's bonkers," said Janet.

"When kids go past her yard," Marzipan said, "she hooks them in with her broom and puts them in a pot and boils them up."

"Don't be daft," said Calvin. "She just shouts at you, that's all."

"Why does she shout then, if she's not a witch?" said Marzipan.

"Because she's deaf, that's why," said Janet. "She don't know she's shouting. She can't hear herself."

Janet had the ball. "Well, *I'm* going," she said. Janet and Calvin ran down the street. Melinda and Marzipan ran after them.

"Well, she is a witch," Marzipan told Melinda.

"*I* know. Let's play rounders," Calvin said.

"We haven't got a bat," said Janet.

"We'll find something on the tip."

It wasn't a real tip. It was a piece of waste ground where the coalman's stables had once been. Old Mr Kelly, the coalman, had still delivered coal with his horse and cart right up until he died. Then the stables and coal sheds had been pulled down. The Council said they were going to make it into a little park with swings and things, but they had never got round to it. So it was just a square of waste ground where children sometimes went to play cricket or football or tig. But

when local people had something to throw out that was too big to fit in the dustbin, under cover of night, they sometimes dumped it there. And that's why it was called the tip.

Calvin soon found a grill pan from an abandoned gas stove. "This'll make a good bat," he said.

Janet found a pram wheel and the leg off a bed. "These'll do for corners," she said. "We need two more corners."

Marzipan found a baby's car seat. Melinda found a kettle with a hole burnt in the bottom.

They put the four corner markers in their places. Janet said, "Me and Calv against you two."

Mazipan said, "That's not fair."

"'Course it is," said Janet.

"I'm not playing," said Marzipan.

"All right," said Janet. "Me and you against Melinda and Calv — bags first bat."

Calvin told Melinda, "When she hits the ball, you've got to run and get it and throw it to me."

"I know," Melinda said.

Janet held the grill pan by the handle. Calvin threw

the Very Bouncy Ball and Janet hit it—CLONK! Up it went into the air, then down, and bounced once, and then—it disappeared over the wall into the witch's back yard. They all looked at each other.

"You go," Calvin said to Janet. "You hit it."

"I'm not going," said Janet.

"You said she wasn't a witch," said Marzipan.

"I don't care," said Janet. "I'm not going. It's not my ball."

"Well, I'm not going," said Calvin.

"Neither am I," said Marzipan.

Melinda was scared. But she wanted her Very Bouncy Ball back. She went over to the witch's yard. She lay on the ground and looked under the gate. But she couldn't see the ball. "Will you give me a bunk up?" she asked.

Calvin cupped his hands together. Melinda stood in Calvin's hands and looked over the wall. "I can see it," she said. "Down by the back door." She climbed over the wall, onto the dustbin, and jumped down into the witch's yard. She got the ball and climbed onto the dustbin again.

"WHAT DO YOU THINK YOU'RE DOING IN MY YARD!"

Melinda looked round and saw the witch coming out of her back door. "I'm getting my Bouncy Ball," she said.

"GET DOWN OFF MY DUSTBIN!" shouted the witch. She came down the yard towards Melinda. Melinda threw the ball over the wall and clambered up, grazing her knees. She jumped down on the other side, stinging her feet, and ran to her friends.

"Where's my ball?" she asked.

"It went in the weeds," Calvin said. He pointed to the tangle of long grass and brambles and fireweed that grew at the top end of the tip.

They watched for a while to see that the witch didn't come out of her gate. Then they began to search for the ball.

"I can't find it," Janet said. "I'm going home."

"So am I," said Marzipan. "I'm not allowed to play down here, anyway."

Calvin stayed for a bit. Then he went too.

Melinda searched for the ball among the rubbish on

her own. Then she went home crying.

Her mum was feeding the baby. "What's the matter, love?" she asked.

"I've lost my Bouncy Ball."

"Have you, dear. Well, don't cry. Turn the kettle off for me, will you." Melinda turned the kettle off. "Come over here," said Mum. She put her arm round Melinda. "Don't upset yourself over a ball."

"But I spent all next week's pocket money on it," Melinda said.

"Never mind. I expect when Saturday comes, your dad'll find some pocket money for you."

"But I've lost my new ball, Mum, and it was ever so smashing."

"Well, I'll tell you what," said her mum. "You get my purse, and I'll see if I've got enough for another one."

"Where's your purse, Mum?" Melinda asked, drying her eyes.

"I don't know, dear," said Melinda's mum. "You'll have to look for it."

— Redecorating —

One evening Melinda's dad announced, "I'm going to redecorate this living-room."

Melinda's mum said, "I'll believe that when I see it."

Dad said, "Just you wait and see."

Mum said, "I'll wait a long time before there's anything to see."

The next Saturday morning, when her mum had gone shopping and taken the baby with her, Melinda said to her dad, "Are we going to do the living-room today?"

"Ooh, I don't know, Melinda," he said. "I've had a hard week at work this week."

"Oh, go on, Dad," Melinda wheedled.

Her dad sighed. "All right, love," he said. "We might as well get it over and done with. I'll go down the shop and buy some wallpaper and paint. Do you want to come?"

Melinda said, "Yes, please."

In the shop they looked through a big book that had wallpaper patterns in. Dad said, "Well, love, what do you think your mother will like?"

There was one pattern with flowers and leaves. Melinda said, "That one."

Dad said, "Do you think five rolls will be enough?"

Melinda said, "Five? It shouldn't need that many."

They bought five rolls of wallpaper and a tin of paint.

When they got home, Brian was asleep in his pram outside the front door. Mum was in the kitchen putting the shopping away. Dad said proudly, "Well, Grace, what do you think of this?"

Mum said, "Oh, Fred, where did you get that wallpaper — out of the Ark?"

Dad said, "We thought you'd like it." Melinda didn't say anything.

Dad asked, "Shall I take it back?"

"You might as well put it up now it's here," Mum said. "If you don't do it while you've got the bug, you won't ever do it at all."

Melinda said, "It looks brighter than this what's on the wall."

"That's true," Mum said. "Anything would look brighter than this."

Mum had brought in the newspaper. Dad sat down in the armchair to read it. Melinda said, "Aren't you going to do the decorating?"

Dad sighed. "All right, love," he said. "Do you want to give me a hand?"

Melinda said, "Coo, yeah."

"Right then," he said. "We'll do the paintwork first. Right-o, Grace. There's two workpeople here who'd like a cup of tea before we start."

Dad tried to open the tin of paint with a two pence piece. But he couldn't get the lid off. Melinda suggested, "Why don't you do it with a knife?"

Dad said, "That's a good idea, love. Fetch one from the kitchen for me, will you?"

He tried to open the tin with the knife. The knife broke. Mum said, "Ooh, I don't know. You're a cack-handed Harry, you are, Fred. Now look what you've done to my knife."

Mum put old newspapers down. She said, "I want the paint on the door, not on the floor."

Dad said, "Yes, dear."

Dad got two paint brushes from the cupboard under the stairs. One for himself and one for Melinda. He let Melinda help him paint the door. She got paint on her hands. She got paint on her clothes. She got paint in her hair.

When her mum saw her she said, "Ooh, just look at you, you messy pup. Why didn't you watch her, Fred? — Ooh, Fred!"

Melinda's dad was all covered with paint as well.

The next Saturday, after breakfast, Melinda said, "Can we do the papering today?"

Dad sighed. "All right, love," he said. "Are you going to help?"

Melinda said, "Yes, please."

Mum said, "Well, try not to make as much mess as

you did last week, the pair of you. I've only just finished cleaning that up."

Melinda helped her dad mix up some paste in a bucket. Her job was stirring it round and round.

They borrowed Mum's scissors and tape measure. Mum said, "And make sure you put them back when you're done. I can never find anything in this house."

They put the table in the middle of the room. They unrolled some paper on the table. Dad measured up the paper. "We need to cut it off here," he said. He couldn't find the scissors. Melinda found them. They were underneath the paper. "Where did I say to cut?" Dad asked.

"Just there," said Melinda, pointing.

She held the paper while he cut it. Then he spread the paste on the paper with a brush. He folded the paper over at the bottom. Then lifted it carefully and climbed up onto a chair. He pressed the wallpaper onto the wall. He smoothed out the bumps with a screwed-up cloth. "There," he said, pleased with himself. "That's the way to do it, love."

Melinda said, "That looks nice."

But when she pulled the bottom of the paper down, it didn't reach the skirting board. They'd cut it short.

Sometimes there was too much paste on the paper. The paper tore. Sometimes there wasn't enough paste on the paper. The paper wouldn't stick on the wall. It fell on Dad's head. Sometimes the paste dried too soon. Where they folded the paper up at the bottom, it got stuck and Melinda couldn't pull it down.

Dad said, "Never mind, love. It won't matter very much a hundred years from now. Let's call it a day and have a cup of tea."

Melinda said, "OK."

Next morning they did some more. They got one lot of wallpaper stuck on the table. Mum said, "Very nice, I'm sure. We must be the only family in the street with a table to match the walls."

Dad said, "Only one more wall to do now. We'll soon be done."

But they had used up all the paper, when they'd only done half the wall.

Mum said, "Well, that looks very nice, that does! I hope you're not going to leave it like that!"

Dad said, "Well, we can't buy any more wallpaper today, Grace. It's Sunday. I think I'll put my feet up. We've earned a rest, haven't we, love?"

Melinda said, "Yes, Dad."

Mum said, "Where's my tape measure? And my scissors?"

Melinda tried to reach them across the table. But she knocked them off into the bucket of paste. Mum said, "Ooh, now look! You're a right couple of messy so-and-sos, you two are."

Aunty Anne came in from up the road to borrow 50p for her meter. "Ooh," she said. "I see you're in the middle of decorating."

Mum said, "Yes. My Melinda and my hubby have done it themselves."

"Yes," said Aunty Anne. "I can see you haven't had men in to do it."

Mum said, "Well, I think it's very nice. I like anything nice and bright. I think they've done very well. Hold the baby a minute, Fred, while I get Anne 50p. Has anybody seen my purse?"

Nobody had.

Melinda found it. It was in the airing cupboard.

When Aunty Anne had gone, Dad said to Melinda, "Next weekend we'll have to get some more paper, love, and finish that wall off."

Mum said, "I'll believe that when I see it."

Dad said, "Just you wait and see."

Mum said, "I'll wait a long time before there's anything to see."

Melinda said, "Never mind, Mum. I'll do it for you. When I'm big."

— That Cat —

One evening, Melinda's dad gave her a kitten. He got it from a man at work. It was tabby, so Melinda called it Tabitha.

When Tabitha was little, she liked to play with the baby's rattle, and Mum's knitting, and pieces of string. One day she tried to climb up Mum's Busy Lizzie plant and tipped it off the window sill. The flower pot smashed on the floor.

Mum said, "That cat will have to go. I've got enough on my plate clearing up after you two and the baby, without a cat as well."

Dad said, "Ah, you couldn't hurt her. She's such a lovely little thing. I'll buy another flower pot from Harry's."

"I'll believe that when I see it," Mum said.

Tabitha used to hide under chairs and spring out like a lion at Mum's legs. Mum said, "Look at the ladders in my tights. That cat will have to go."

Dad said, "Never mind, Grace. I'll see if I can get you some new tights off young Sid."

"That'll be the day," Mum said.

One morning Tabitha rubbed herself round Mum's legs and tripped her, causing her to drop the breakfast bowls on the kitchen floor. There was broken crockery and porridge everywhere. Mum said, "Now look what she's done. That cat will have to go."

Dad said, "But she's a good friend for our Melinda. I'll get some new breakfast bowls down the market tomorrow."

"Yes," Mum said, "and pigs might fly."

As Tabitha grew older she didn't play so much any more. But she ate more cat food. And she drank more milk. Mum said, "That cat will eat us out of house and home. That cat will have to go."

Dad said, "A cat's got to eat, dear. I'll get a carton of cat food cheap from the Cash and Carry."

Mum said, "If you earned a pound, Fred, for every one of your good intentions, we'd be millionaires."

Tabitha kept on getting fatter and fatter. Then one day, fat Tabitha waddled into the cupboard under the stairs, and wouldn't come out when Melinda called. She didn't even come when Melinda rattled her saucer at tea time. Then, when she did come out, what a surprise — she was thin!

Melinda fetched the torch from her dad's bike, and crawled into the cupboard. In a cardboard box at the very back, she found four kittens, all in a heap. Three were tabby, and one was ginger. Their eyes were closed tight, and when Melinda picked them up, they squeaked.

When Tabitha heard them, she climbed back into the box. She licked them all over, one by one, then lay down on her side. The four kittens scrambled over each other and sucked milk from her teats, and Tabitha closed her eyes and purred.

Melinda called her mum and dad. Mum said, "I'm not feeding five. That cat will have to go."

Dad said, "But she'll feed the babies herself, Grace.

And when they're bigger, we'll put an ad in Harry's shop window — *Free to good home.* Meantime, we'd better order an extra pint of milk off the milkman. Feeding babies is thirsty work.''

"A fat lot you'd know about that, Fred," Mum said.

Melinda gave the kittens names. Dopey, Sleepy and Scratchy were tabby, and Perky was ginger. When they were eight weeks old, she gave three of the kittens away to her friends. She gave Dopey to Janet. She gave Sleepy to Calvin. And she gave Scratchy to Tom. But nobody seemed to want a kitten that was ginger. Melinda was pleased: Perky was her favourite.

Mum said, "We can't afford to keep two. That cat will have to go."

Dad said, "Ah, you couldn't harm him. He's such a pretty little thing. And two don't cost much more than one."

"How do you know it's a 'him'?" Mum said.

"Ginger cats are usually toms," Dad said.

"Not always," said Mum.

"Nearly always," Dad said.

Perky liked to play with the baby's toys, and Mum's knitting, and milk bottle tops. One day he was boxing the leaves of Mum's new spider plant, and he pulled it off the window sill and the flower pot smashed on the floor. He used to hide under chairs and spring out like a lion at people's legs. Mum started wearing trousers around the house because she said it cost her too much for tights.

Perky was always leaping onto Tabitha, clawing her tail and biting her fur. In the mornings both cats rubbed themselves around everybody's legs and tripped them all.

But after a while Perky didn't seem so playful any more. He started getting fatter. Melinda didn't know what could be the matter. But she heard her mum say to her dad, "That cat will have to go."

And Dad said, "Yes, dear."

46

— The Street Play —

Melinda had to look after the baby while her mum got the washing done. Playing with Brian was good fun at first, but then she got bored. When the washing was finished, Mum said, "Thank you, love. Take 10p out of my purse and get yourself a lolly."

"Coo, ta, Mum," Melinda said. "Where's your purse?"

"I don't know, dear," her mum said. "You'll have to look for it."

Melinda searched high and low. She searched here, there and everywhere. But she couldn't find her mum's purse anywhere. Melinda got fed up, so she went out to play.

Some big boys were playing football. The goal was the terrace-end wall. Calvin was the goalie. "Can I play, Calvin?" Melinda asked.

"No," he said. "You're too little. Get out of the way."

Some girls were playing hopscotch. Marzipan and Janet were playing. Marzipan was picking up the slate. She was standing on one leg. "Can I play, Marz?" Melinda asked.

"Shut up," Marzipan said. "You're putting me off."

"Can I play, Janet?" Melinda asked.

"No," she said. "There's too many already."

Tom was playing marbles with Phil. Melinda knew Tom wouldn't let her play. "Hiya, Tom," she said.

Tom ignored her. Tom rolled his marble. His marble hit Phil's. "Got it!" he shouted.

"Good shot, Tom," Melinda said.

Tom pretended he didn't hear. Phil said, "Get lost, Carrot Top!"

Little Kathy was playing dollies on her doorstep. Melinda stood watching her. She wanted to join in, but she was afraid that if she played with little Kathy, her friends would call her a baby.

Then she heard a noise. Like a big drum beating. Like a band. The noise was getting louder. The big boys stopped playing football. The girls stopped playing hopscotch. Tom and Phil stopped playing marbles. Only little Kathy went on playing with her dolls as if she hadn't heard. Everyone else stood still to listen.

"What's that?"

"It's a band."

"It's coming closer."

"Come on."

Everybody (except little Kathy) started to run. They ran round the corner past Harry's shop. They ran down the street. The big boys were in front. When they neared the next corner by the main road, they all stopped. A band was coming round the corner. Not a works' band. Not an army band. Not the Boys' Brigade band. It was more like a clowns' band.

All the people in the band wore funny clothes. They had masks or make-up on their faces. One had a big drum. One had a little drum. One had a cymbal. One had a washboard. One had a rattle. One had a hooter.

One had a piece of pipe on a string. One had a hub cap off a car wheel.

They were all banging a rhythm. They were all singing:

> "Follow the music.
> Follow the music.
> The music of the band.
> The music of the band.
> Come and see the play.
> Come and see the play.
> Let me take you by the hand.
> Let me take you by the hand.
> Come and see the good men.
> Come and see the bad men.
> Come and see the funny men.
> Come and see the sad men.
> Follow the music.
> Follow the music.
> The music of the band."

A crowd was following the band. There were lots of children. There were grown-ups pushing babies in prams. There were little kids in push chairs. There were kids sitting on their dads' shoulders. Old people came out of their doors. They wanted to see what all the noise was about. A big black dog was barking at the people in the band.

More people joined the crowd. Melinda joined, with the other kids from her street. They all followed the band. They went round the corner. They went up the street. They went onto the piece of waste ground they called the tip. It was right near the witch's house. But Melinda didn't care. No one was bothered about that. The band stopped playing. The band people put down their instruments. Everyone waited to see what would happen.

"Hello, everybody," a man shouted. "Do you want to see a play?"

"Yes," they all shouted back.

"Give us a bit of space, then," he said. "Don't all push forward. Let the little ones come to the front. Sit down on the ground — then the play will begin."

The play was about the Winter King. He kept the Spring Princess locked in prison. The prison was guarded by a henchman. Then the Summer King fought the henchman. The henchman ran away, and the Summer King let the princess out of the prison. But the henchman went and told the Winter King. The Winter King was very angry. He shouted:

"I am the Winter King.
I rule the ice, the snow, the frost.
When I freeze the world,
The Summer King is lost!"

Then the two kings had a fight. The Summer King asked all the children to help him win. He asked them to shout:

"Sun King, Sun King,
Turn on the heat.
Then we'll see
That Ice King beat!"

In the end the Summer King won. He breathed fire out of his mouth, and the Winter King ran away.

Then the actors talked to the children. The Spring Princess spoke to Melinda. "What's your name?" she asked.

Melinda told her.

"Her name's Carrot Top," Tom said.

"Did you like the play?" the princess asked Melinda.

"Coo, yeah," Melinda said. "It was smashing."

"You have got lovely hair," the princess said. "I wish I had hair like you. I wouldn't need a crown then. My hair would be my crowning glory."

Melinda didn't say anything out loud, but she felt pleased, and pretty, and special. *Crowning glory,* she thought to herself. *Crowning glory.* And she relished the phrase, like a mouthful of juicy peach.

"Do you want us to come back next week?" the princess asked.

"Yes, please."

"Listen for the band then. We've got to go now. See you."

The actors picked up their instruments and started to bang their rhythm. Then they marched off, singing their song. Everyone followed them to the main road. Then the band people stopped playing and waved goodbye.

As the children walked back to their street, Tom said, "Weren't that great."

Phil said, "Yeah, let's play the Summer King. Bags I the Summer King."

"All right," said Tom, grudgingly. "Bags I the Winter King."

Melinda was the Spring Princess.

She didn't need a crown. Her hair was her crowning glory.

It was a great game.

Mad Max and
— the Grazer —

One Saturday afternoon, Melinda's mum wanted some peace and quiet while the baby was asleep, so Melinda's dad took Melinda to the fête. There were lots of games and things to do, and a raffle and a lucky dip, and stalls, higgledy-piggledy, all over the place. Stalls with plants, and cakes, and books, and toys, and face paints, and pictures, and pancakes, and nick-nacks, and bric-a-brac.

When they got home, Dad made a pot of tea and put his feet up. Melinda decided to have a stall of her own. She took the folding table out of the cupboard under the stairs, and set it up outside the front door. She went up to her bedroom, and collected all her toys and

all her books. She had to go upstairs seven times to get
them all. Then she waited for her first customer.

Some Indian ladies came by, but they didn't stop to
look. Squint-eyed Jim came along, but he couldn't see

what was for sale. Jamaica Joe passed by on the other side of the road. "What are you up to, Melinda?" he called.

"Selling things on my stall," she told him.

"You'll have Harry after you," he laughed. "You'll be taking all his trade."

Then Tom came along. "Do you want to buy something off my stall?" Melinda asked him.

"No," he said. "I'm going to the site."

Along by the canal, where the mill used to be, there was a building site where a little housing estate was sprouting up.

"You're not supposed to go there," Melinda told him.

"*I* don't care."

"My mum said it's not safe."

"Well, *I*'m going. It's good. Are you coming? Or are you too scared?"

"I'm not scared."

"Well, come on then."

"All right," Melinda said. She didn't want Tom to think she was a baby.

They went up to the top of the street. They climbed over the wall, and went along by the canal to the building site. Even though it was a Saturday the men were still working there. There was a knock-knock-knocking sound. There was the growl of a big machine. It was very noisy.

"Mad Max works here," Tom said.

"Who's Mad Max?" Melinda asked.

"He's the man who drives the grazer."

"What's a grazer?"

"A big yellow thing," Tom said. "Don't you know anything! Mad Max chases you in his grazer. So when he comes — we scarper."

Melinda looked all around, but she couldn't see a Mad Max anywhere. There were heaps of sand. There were square stacks of bricks. There were lengths of pipe and piles of tiles. They climbed to the top of a gravel mountain. "We're the kings of the castle," Melinda sang to some workmen who were pushing barrows past. "You're the dirty rascals." But the workmen didn't take any notice.

They watched a man climb up a ladder carrying a

load of tiles. He began putting tiles on the roof. The
tiles were like waves. A cement mixer lorry came by.
Then a lorry loaded with bricks.

Melinda heard a powerful engine start up behind
her. She looked round.

"That's the grazer," Tom said.

It was yellow and big. It had red wheels and a red scoop. It had a bulldozer at one end and an arm at the other. It held its arm in the air like a clenched fist. There was a black man in the driver's seat.

"That's Mad Max," Tom said.

The grazer moved slowly and jerkily towards them. The engine strained and screamed. Mad Max leaned out of his cab and shouted something.

"Scarper!" Tom yelled.

They ran all the way back to Melinda's house. They were so hot they went into the kitchen for a drink of orange squash. Then they went out to Melinda's stall.

"Roll up!" she shouted, once she'd got her breath back. "Come and buy from my stall."

Marzipan came from over the road. "How much is that rabbit?" she asked.

"50p," Melinda said.

"Haven't got no money," Marzipan said, and went away again.

Calvin came from up the street. "How much is that Batcopter?" he asked.

"50p," Melinda said.

"Haven't got 50p," he said.

Then they saw Mad Max coming. Tom scarpered.

"Hello, Carrot Top," said Mad Max to Melinda. "What we got here?" He was looking friendly.

"It's a stall," Melinda said.

"It's a very good stall," he replied. "It's better than the shopping centre. I hope you get a lot of customers."

"Yes," said Melinda. "I hope so too."

Mad Max looked at Melinda with big, serious dark brown eyes. "Did I see you over the building site a little while back?" he asked.

Melinda moistened her lips with her tongue. "Yes."

"I thought so. That's why I came this way. Did you tell your mother where you were going?"

Melinda looked down at her muddy shoes. "No."

"You should always tell your mother or father."

Melinda bit her lip. "I know."

"And you shouldn't play up there."

Melinda twiddled her fingers. "I know."

"It's dangerous. We wouldn't want any of you kids to get hurt."

Melinda looked up at Max. He smiled and nodded his head. And Melinda nodded hers.

"I'm not going to go there any more," she promised.

"Good. Anyway, I have to hurry home now — or Lovelace will give me some bad talking."

"I know a Lovelace," Melinda said. "She's in Mrs Tripp's class at school."

Mad Max beamed. "That's my little girl," he said. "Whose class are you in?"

"Mr Domingo's."

"I know Mr Domingo."

"We call him Porky," Melinda said.

Mad Max laughed, then looked at his watch. "I'm late," he said, "for a very important date. On Saturdays I have to take Lovelace to her granny's for tea. I'll tell her to look out for you at school. What's your name?"

"Melinda."

"Right, Melinda. I'll tell her." And Mad Max hurried away down the road, turning once to smile and wave before disappearing round the corner at the bottom of the street.

After Mad Max had gone, Tom came back. Calvin and Phil and Marzipan were with him. "What'd he say?" Tom wanted to know.

"Oh, we just talked," Melinda said casually. "He's my friend."

Seeing the crowd around the stall, more kids came along. "How much is this tractor?" asked Janet.

"50p," Melinda said.

"That's too much," Janet said. "It's only second hand."

"How much you got?" asked Melinda.

"Nothing," Janet said.

"All right," Melinda said. "You can have it for nothing."

Then the others wanted something for nothing too. They ran and told their friends. Soon there were lots of kids. They bought armfuls of things. Melinda was doing great business. Until in the end there was nothing left. She folded up the table and put it back under the stairs, and went in for tea.

After tea, Mum put the baby to bed, and went to bingo with Granny Gray. Melinda watched telly and played with her dad. He gave her a horse ride on his back. He gave her a flying aeroplane on his feet. Then it was time for bed. Melinda got undressed and brushed her teeth. Then her dad came up to tuck her up in bed. He looked around her room.'

"Where's all your things?" he asked.

"I had a stall," Melinda said. "Just like at the fête."

"But where's your toys and books?"

"Sold them," she said.

"You sold them?" he said. "All of them?"

"Yes."

"Where's all the money?" he asked.

"I didn't get any money," she said. "The children were too poor."

"You mean you gave everything away?" he said.

"Oh, no," she said. "I sold them on my stall."

"But you got no money?"

"No," she said.

"Where's your big teddy?" he asked.

"I sold it."

"Who to?"

"Can't remember."

"You've got nothing left!" he said. He was angry now. "Look! Everything gone! All them things cost money! I had to work hard to buy them things! Now you've got nothing left to play with! And that was a lovely teddy!"

He looked upset. Melinda began to cry. "I'm sorry, Dad," she said. "I didn't mean to."

"Never mind," he said. "Don't cry." He tucked her into bed and lay down and cuddled her. "I'm sorry I got angry," he said. "One minute I'm telling you not to be greedy and selfish, and the next minute I'm telling you off for being generous and kind. It'll soon be your birthday. You'll get some presents then. Shall I tell you a true story?"

"Yes, please," said Melinda.

"When I was little, I always wanted a teddy. And I never had one. So when you were born, I bought you the teddy I would have liked. And now he's gone. So you see, I wasn't upset because of what you did — but because of what happened to me. I expect one of your friends is cuddling Ted in bed right now, just like I'm cuddling you. You're a lovely girl. Dry your eyes and tell me what adventures you've had today."

So Melinda told her dad about Mad Max and the Grazer.

— The Invitation —

Melinda's mum said Melinda had to go to bed. "Oh, Mum," Melinda pleaded. "Five more minutes."

"I just let you have an extra quarter of an hour, you cheeky madam. Up to bed this minute."

But just then, there was a knock on the front door and Melinda's cousin Sandra came in. Sandra was ever so grown up. She was eighteen. And Melinda thought she was lovely. She had fine, straight, black hair cut short. Melinda wished she had hair like that, then she wouldn't get teased so much.

Sandra was flushed and excited. "Hello, all," she said.

"You're looking pleased with yourself," said Mum.

"If your smile gets any bigger, your face will fall in half," Dad said.

"You look like the cat that ate the cream," added Mum.

"Ooh, Aunty, I'm ever so thrilled," Sandra said. "I'm going to get married."

"Who to?" asked Dad.

"Errol, of course," said Sandra, pouting. "Who d'you think?"

"Well, he's a lucky feller," Dad said. "If I was ten years younger he wouldn't have got the chance."

"Don't you kid yourself, Fred," Mum said. "She wouldn't have looked twice at you."

"Coo, Sandra," Melinda said. "You are lucky. Can I come to the wedding?"

"Don't you be so saucy," Mum said. "You wait till you're invited."

"Of course you can come to the wedding," Sandra said to Melinda. "I wouldn't get married at all if you couldn't be there."

Melinda felt herself blush — she felt so pleased.

"When's it going to be?" asked Dad.

"Next month," Sandra said.

"Next month?" echoed Mum. "That's a bit sudden, isn't it?"

"Young love can't wait," Dad said.

"A fat lot you'd know about young love," said Mum.

"I wish it was this month," Sandra said. "I'm going to have a white dress and the bridesmaids will be in pink."

"And is Errol going to wear a top hat?" Dad asked, laughing.

"No," said Sandra. "He said he'd feel silly in one of them."

"He'd *look* silly in one of them," Dad said.

"Not half so silly as you would," Mum said, and they all laughed.

When Sandra had gone, Melinda said, "Can I be one of Sandra's bridesmaids?"

"Of course not," said Mum. "She'd have asked you if she'd wanted you. I expect she'll have her sisters do it."

"But they're grown up," Melinda protested.

"That's got nothing to do with it," Mum said. "And I

thought I told you ages ago to get up to bed. Just look at the time. And don't be making a noise or you'll wake Brian."

Melinda felt very sad. But when she was in bed her dad came up to tuck her in and say good night. "It's a good job I did some overtime last week," he said. "We'll have to go shopping on Saturday and get you a new dress and new shoes and everything. We'll get you kitted out in a complete new outfit: you'll be the star of the wedding — after the bride, that is."

"Coo, thanks, Dad," Melinda said.

On Friday evening Melinda was watching *Cartoon Time* when Dad came in from work. He didn't take his boots off at the door like he usually did, or hang his coat up. He just slumped down in the armchair. Mum was sitting in the other armchair feeding Brian.

"Get your dad a cup of tea, Melinda," Mum said.

"Oh, Mum," Melinda complained. "It's nearly finished."

"Don't be so selfish," Mum said. "Dad's been working hard all day. He's tired out."

"Let her watch her cartoon," Dad said. "It'll be over in a minute."

"Dinner won't be long, Fred. Oh, Brian! Stop it!" Brian was blowing bubbles with his food and a brown mess had spread all over his face. Dad didn't say anything. "Well, what's the matter with you?" Mum asked him. "You look like a wet weekend."

"I'm sorry, love," Dad said. Melinda stopped watching the television and looked at her dad. He sounded upset.

"Whatever's the matter, Fred?" Mum asked.

"I got laid off. Because of the cuts. They're laying off six of us — the last to come, the first to go."

"Oh, Fred. What are we going to do now?"

"I don't know, Grace. Back on the dole, I suppose."

"Something will turn up, Fred. Something always does."

"There's nothing, Grace. Not for someone without skills, like me. They finished us off early. I've just been down the Job Centre now."

"Does that mean I can't have my new dress?" Melinda asked.

"I'm sorry, Melinda." Dad shook his head. "None of us will be getting anything new for a while now."

"I don't want to go to the wedding at all, then," Melinda said sulkily.

"Don't be silly," Mum said. "There's lots of jumbles on tomorrow. We'll find you something nice, just you see."

Melinda felt so unhappy she was about to burst into tears, but Brian chose that moment to turn his bowlful of dinner upside down, like a hat, on top of his head.

"Oh, Brian!" Mum cried.

There was brown squelch in his hair, and brown squelch running down his face. Brian beamed proudly and began to laugh. Dad began to laugh too. Then Mum laughed. And finally Melinda forgot about crying and laughed as well. And the room was full of laughter.

The following morning Sandra came round. Melinda was in the kitchen helping her mum. "I've come to see Melinda," she heard Sandra say to Dad. Melinda hurried into the living-room. "Hi, Carrots," she said. She was still as excited as she had been earlier in the week — like someone at the fair who's just come off the water chute and is going on the big dipper. "Can you come to the dressmaker? Quick. Right now. This minute."

"What for?" Melinda asked.

"To be measured for your bridesmaid's dress, of course."

"Oh, Sandra." Melinda jumped up and down with

delight. "Am I going to be your bridesmaid?"

"Of course you are. And Loretta's going to be the other one."

"Who's Loretta?"

"Errol's little sister. I think she's a bit younger than you, but you're both about the same size."

"But Sandra," Melinda said. "I don't think we can afford a dress. Dad's on the dole."

"You don't have to pay for it, silly," Sandra said. "It's my wedding. Uncle Norman will pay for it. Come on. Hurry up."

The dressmaker made the girls try on some dresses to see what would suit them. Sandra had chosen pink. Melinda thought the dress was beautiful. It looked lovely on Loretta, who had shiny, black, curly hair. But when the dressmaker looked at Melinda she said, "Oh, dear. You can't wear pink with that hair." Melinda felt ashamed. She looked down at the floor and tried not to cry. "What about a nice rich cream?" the dressmaker suggested. So Melinda tried on a cream dress.

"I like that much better than the pink," Errol said.

"And it suits Melinda to a T," Sandra said.

"Yes," added Errol. "And it's much more classy."

And the wedding day was wonderful. And late that night, when Melinda's dad was putting her to bed, he said, "I was proud of you, today, chickadee. Everybody kept saying, 'Who's that lovely little bridesmaid with the bright red hair?'"

"Did they honestly?" Melinda asked.

"Honestly," her dad said. "You were the star of the show — after the bride, of course."

— Melinda's Birthday —

Calvin, Janet, Marzipan and Tom were doing stunts on their bikes. They were practising wheelies, and they'd got some bricks and planks and had made jumps. "Hiya, Carrot Top," Calvin called as he glided by, standing on his saddle.

Melinda ran indoors. Dad was reading a library book. "Will you get my bike out of the shed, Dad?" Melinda asked.

"Can I just finish this chapter?" he asked.

"Oh, no, Dad," pleaded Melinda. "They'll finish their game and I won't be able to play."

Dad sighed. "No peace for the wicked," he said. He got up and they went out into the back yard. Mum was standing at the back gate, holding Brian. She was talking to Aunty Anne and Granny Gray and Old Mother Hammer.

The shed had once been an outside toilet. Now it was full of all sorts of junk. And in the middle of all the junk was Melinda's little bicycle. Her dad had got it second hand when she was small, and he had run up and down the road with her teaching her to ride it.

"There you are," Dad said, setting the bike down on the ground. "Can I go back to my book now?"

"Oh, Dad," Melinda said. "It's got a puncture."

Dad sighed again. "Are you any good at punctures, Grace?" he asked.

"No, I'm not," Mum said. "I've got enough on my plate without worrying about punctures."

"I should have thought that was a man's job," Aunty Anne put in.

"We don't have men's jobs and women's jobs here," Dad said. "We're very modern in this house. Grace and I like to share everything."

Mum turned right round and looked at Dad with a surprised expression. "You cheeky saucebox," she said. "That's the first I heard of it."

"Well, it's the thought that counts," Dad said.

"They're all the same, these men," Aunty Anne grumbled. "I wouldn't give one house room."

Mum turned back to face her. "I wouldn't be without my Fred," she said. "He's worth his weight in gold."

Dad winked at Melinda. "Well, what are we going to do about this then?" he said.

"Have we got a puncture repair kit?" Melinda asked.

"No. Go and see if Harry sells them."

He didn't. But Jamaica Joe was in the shop, and he had one — a brand new one. He'd sold his old car that was always going wrong and bought himself a racing bike. He'd bought a repair kit too, just in case. "I like to be prepared for the worst," Jamaica Joe told Melinda. "That's what living in this country has taught me. Go on up to the house and ask Hyacinth to give it to you. Tell her it's in the kitchen drawer with the string. And be sure you bring it back when you've done with it."

"I'm going to get my bike out," Melinda called to Calvin who rode past sitting on the handlebars, facing backwards.

Melinda helped Dad take the wheel off her bike and get the inner tube out. They held the inner tube in a bowl of water and the bubbles told them where the hole was. When the puncture was mended they had to force the inner tube under the tyre with spoons and then put the wheel back on.

"I'll do your brakes and tighten the chain while we're about it," Dad said.

"Oh, Dad," Melinda complained, "the game will be over before I get out there."

"You can't ride a bike unless it's safe," Dad said.

Dad struggled with spanners and screwdrivers and pliers while Melinda waited around impatiently. "It's your birthday next week," Dad said suddenly.

"I know," Melinda said.

"And you know I'm on the dole, don't you?"

"Yes, Dad."

"And you know that means we won't be able to get you very much for your birthday, don't you?"

"Yes, Dad."

"It's not because we don't love you."

"I know, Dad."

"There we are," he said. "Try that."

"The brakes don't work at all now," Melinda said. "And the chain's looser than it was before."

"Oh, I am sorry, Melinda," Dad said. "Still, they'll do for now."

"But Dad," Melinda said. "The tyre's still got a puncture in."

"Oh, dear," Dad said. "I must have pinched the tube trying to get it back in. I'll have to start all over again."

While Dad had another go at repairing the puncture, Melinda went out onto the street to see how the game was getting on. But there were no bikes in sight. The game had ended. There were no kids out now. They'd all gone in for their lunch.

Melinda went back into her yard. "You needn't bother, Dad," she said. "There's no one playing out any more."

"We might as well finish, now we've started," Dad said. But when he tried to put the wheel back onto the bike he stripped the thread inside the nut. "Oh, dear," he said. "I'll get a new nut on Monday. Not to worry."

"Anyway," Melinda told him, "the tyre's still flat."

Just then, Mum poked her head out of the back door. "Come and wash your hands, you two. Haven't you done that puncture yet, Fred?"

"Well, we've sort of done it," Dad said. "Haven't we, Melinda?"

Mum and Melinda looked at each other and shook their heads.

Monday was a good day. Melinda was looking after Brian while Mum was getting the tea. Mum was singing with the records on the radio. Melinda piled up Brian's plastic, coloured beakers, and Brian knocked them down again and squealed with pleasure. Then Dad came bursting in.

First he plucked Brian up off the carpet and, singing out of tune and at the top of his voice, twirled him round and round. Then he plonked Brian down and picked up Melinda and danced up and down with her. Then he grabbed Mum, who'd come in from the kitchen to see what all the palaver was about, and did a jig with her all around the room.

"What on earth's got into you, Fred?" Mum kept

saying. "Stop it, will you. Let me go. You're like a dog with two tails."

"Well, there's some life in the old dog yet," Dad said. "Good news, Grace. I've got a job."

"Oh, lovely, Fred. You are clever."

Melinda picked up Brian and danced around with him. "Daddy's got a job, Daddy's got a job," she chanted.

"Ob," echoed Brian and clapped his hands.

Dad stopped dancing and collapsed into a chair. "I'm a gardener," he announced.

"A gardener," Mum repeated, looking doubtful. "What do you know about gardening, Fred?"

"Nothing," said Dad.

"Look what happened when you had that allotment," Mum said. "Even your carrots had club foot."

"Club root, Mum," Melinda informed her. "Not club foot."

"Well, whatever it was, we couldn't eat them," Mum said. "And the only other thing you managed to grow was prize weeds."

"Well, it's a good job," Dad said. "It doesn't pay a

lot, but we'll be better off than we are now. And I'll be working outside, in the fresh air. I like watching things grow."

"I think you'll have to do more than watch them, Fred," Mum said.

Melinda's birthday was on Saturday. When she got up in the morning there were some birthday cards for her. That was good. But there were no presents. Melinda remembered that her dad had said she wouldn't get much this year — but she had thought there would be *something*. Melinda felt rather sad. But her mum and dad seemed not to notice.

After lunch, Dad said, "I want you to come to Grandad's with me."

"What for?" Melinda wanted to know.

"To fetch something," Dad said.

"All that way!" protested Melinda. "Oh, Dad."

"It won't take long," Dad said. "Jamaica Joe's lending me his new bicycle, and we'll go along the canal towpath."

"Do I *have* to go?" Melinda asked.

88

"Yes," Dad said. "You do."

It was very uncomfortable riding all that way on a cross-bar, especially along the bumpy canal path. Melinda was very glad when they arrived, but she wasn't looking forward to the ride back. Dad let himself into Grandad's house with a key.

"Where's Grandad?" Melinda asked.

"He's not here," Dad said. "But there's something for you in his front room."

"Something for me?"

"Yes. Something for a very special birthday girl from her mum and dad."

Melinda's heart beat faster with excitement. She opened the door and looked in. And there in the middle of the room stood the most beautiful, yellow and red, brand new bike — the sort that was just right for jumps and stunts. Melinda stood and stared. "Oh, Dad," she said. "Oh, Dad."

"It's from me and mum," Dad told her.

And Melinda's surprises weren't over. She and Dad rode back along by the canal. When they arrived home Melinda rushed in to say thank you to her mum. But as soon as she got inside the door she was met with a loud chorus of "Happy Birthday to you." And even though some of the singers said, "Dear Carrot Top," Melinda didn't mind. Sandra was there with Errol, and Grandad was there, and Granny Gray, and Aunty Anne (who'd invited herself), and Tom, and Janet, and Calvin, and Marzipan, and Phil, and little Kathy, and of course, most important of all, Mum and Brian. It was the best birthday party Melinda had ever had.

When everyone had gone home, Dad said, "I'm parched, Grace. How about a nice cup of tea?"

"You'll have to wait, Fred. I've got all this washing up to do. And the baby needs bathing, and I don't know what."

"Leave the washing up. Me and the birthday girl will do that later, won't we, my lovely?"

Melinda looked a bit glum. It was her birthday, after all.

"And I'll see to Brian," Dad went on.

"Well, don't start chucking him about like you usually do. He's put away enough ice-cream, jelly and trifle to feed a regiment. He'll be sick before the evening's out."

"I never met a child yet who got sick on ice-cream, jelly and trifle," Dad said. "That's a grown-ups' myth, that is."

Dad picked Brian up and threw him up to the ceiling and caught him again. Brian laughed with delight.

"Well, don't say I didn't warn you," Mum said.

"This is what I used to do to you, Melinda," Dad said. "Your mum used to have a heart attack—she used to think I was going to drop you."

"Do it now," Melinda said.

"You've got to be joking," Dad said. "I can hardly lift you off the ground, let alone throw you up in the air."

Dad held Brian on his hip and pushed the unruly blond curls out of the baby's eyes. Melinda went to Dad and hugged him. "Let's do a hugger-mugger," she said.

"Come on, Grace," Dad said. "A hugger-mugger for Melinda's birthday." He hoisted Melinda onto his other hip. Mum came over and they put their arms round one another like a family of octopuses. They began chanting and circling, slowly at first, then gradually faster and faster, "Hugger-mugger, hugger-mugger, hugger-mugger, hugger-mugger," round and round and round and round until they couldn't speak or twirl any faster, and then stopped and squeezed and cuddled, letting out a great cry of pleasure and love.

"I feel dizzy now," Mum said, breaking away. "I can hardly stand up."

Dad lowered Melinda to the floor. "Thanks for a lovely birthday," she said. Then she ran to her mum and hugged her. "Thanks for a lovely birthday, Mum."

"She's a good kid, our Melinda, isn't she?" Dad said to Mum. "She's the best."

"She certainly is," Mum said.

Brian made a noise which sounded like 'est'. "Hear that," Dad said excitedly. "Even your brother says you're the best."

"Oh, dear," Mum said. "We're out of milk. Melinda, run over to Harry's and get a bottle — there's a dear. Take some money out of my purse."

"Where's your purse, Mum?" Melinda asked.

"I don't know, dear," her mum said. "You'll have to look for it."

The Fiend Next Door

Sheila Lavelle

Charlie Ellis lives next door to Angela Mitchell whom she once described in a class essay as 'My Best Fiend'. Living next to Angela is a mixed blessing. Angela has the most remarkable ideas and somehow Charlie always seems to get involved. The trouble is that Angela's plans have a horrible habit of going badly wrong and more often than not it seems to be Charlie who ends up getting the blame. It was, after all, Angela who borrowed the baby and pretended that she had kidnapped it but it was Charlie who got landed with looking after it – and trying to put it back. Also Angela is not above a little deviousness when it suits her. She certainly stopped at nothing to get her hands on the bag that Charlie had been given though, in the end, Charlie got her own back with vengeance.

Terrible though Angela can be, Charlie has to admit that life would be very dull without her around.

Also in Lions are *My Best Fiend* and *Trouble with the Fiend*.

Simon and the Witch

Margaret Stuart Barry

Simon's friend the witch lives in a neat, semi-detached house with a television and a telephone, but she has never heard of Christmas or been to the seaside. However, she has a wand, which she loses, causing confusion at the local constabulary, and a mean-looking cat called George, who eats the furniture when she forgets to feed him. The witch shows Simon how to turn the school gardener into a frog, and she and her relations liven up a hallowe'en party to the delight of the children and the alarm of the local dignitaries. With a witch for a friend, Simon discovers, life is never dull.

Very highly recommended by ILEA's *Contact* magazine: '. . . who could resist such a lively character?'

You will find more adventures of Simon and the Witch in *The Return of the Witch*, and *The Witch of Monopoly Manor* and *The Witch on Holiday*, all in Lions.

The Reluctant Dragon

Kenneth Grahame

'I *can't* fight and I *won't* fight. Besides, I haven't an enemy in
the world,' the dragon announced firmly.

And he did so want a peaceful life. To write sonnets and find
a place in Society was all he asked. So why did the whole town
insist that he battle with St George, who was such a nice fellow
anyway?

Flossie Teacake's Fur Coat
Flossie Teacake – Again!

Hunter Davies

What Flossie wanted most in the world was to be a teenager like her sister Bella, to be tall and thin and wear make-up and jangling earrings and dye her hair pink.

Flossie, ten years old, tries on Bella's fur coat, and suddenly all her dreams begin to come true. A series of wonderful adventures for Flossie, exuberantly told and matched by Laurence Hutchins's lively illustrations.

Patricia Reilly Giff

The Beast in Ms Rooney's Room
Fish Face
The Pop Corn Contest
December Secrets
In the Dinosaur's Paw
The Valentine Star

Illustrated by Blanche Sims

Meet the kids of the Polk Street School, and in particular the kids in Ms Rooney's class.

Among them are Richard "Beast" Best, who has been kept back a year and is feeling a bit miserable; Emily Arrow, who is a poor reader but a fast runner; Dawn Tiffanie Bosco, the new girl, whom Emily isn't quite sure about to begin with; and chubby Jill Simon, the crybaby. Well, that's what Emily says.

Something is happening every month in their class, like having a popcorn contest, a ride in the fire engine, measuring up dinosaurs, or making presents for special friends.

Read all about what Ms Rooney's class gets up to. And there are more stories to come!

All these books are available at your local bookshop or newsagent, or can be ordered from the publishers.

To order direct from the publishers just tick the titles you want and fill in the form below:

Name _____

Address _____

_____

Send to: Collins Children's Cash Sales
PO Box 11
Falmouth
Cornwall
TR10 9EN

Please enclose a cheque or postal order or debit my Visa/Access –

Credit card no:

Expiry date:

Signature:

– to the value of the cover price plus:

UK: 80p for the first book, and 20p per copy for each additional book ordered to a maximum charge of £2.00.

BFPO: 80p for the first book, and 20p per copy for each additional book.

Overseas and Eire: £1.50 for the first book, £1.00 for the second book, thereafter 30p per book.

Young Lions reserve the right to show new retail prices on covers which may differ from those previously advertised in the text or elsewhere.

Young Lions

The Sleepover Club

The Sleepover
Club Bridesmaids

by Angie Bates

Collins

An imprint of HarperCollinsPublishers

Sleepover Kit List

1. Sleeping bag
2. Pillow
3. Pyjamas or a nightdress
4. Slippers
5. Toothbrush, toothpaste, soap etc
6. Towel
7. Teddy
8. A creepy story
9. Food for a midnight feast:
   chocolate, crisps, sweets, biscuits.
   In fact anything you like to eat.
10. Torch
11. Hairbrush
12. Hair things like a bobble or hairband,
    if you need them
13. Clean knickers and socks
14. Change of clothes for the next day
15. Sleepover diary and membership card

CHAPTER ONE

Yikes! You really made me jump then. I thought it was one of the others coming upstairs.

I left them all watching a video. Actually, I started out watching it too, but Kenny said she couldn't concentrate with me sitting next to her. She said she could FEEL me fizzing, like a Disprin in water.

Well, can you blame me for being a bit fidgety, after the incredible day I just had? (Actually, better make that incredible *week*!!)

Anyway, I didn't want to spoil the film for everyone. Also to be honest, I really needed some peace and quiet. So I came up here to write in my diary. Don't laugh, but in the run up to Mum and Andy's Big Day, I've been keeping two diaries – my official Sleepover Club diary *and* a mega-secret Wedding Diary.

I'm not joking – I've been under stress like you wouldn't believe. There were times when letting off steam in my Wedding Diary was the only thing which kept me sane. Unfortunately, it was practically impossible to find the privacy to actually *write* in it – that's how mad it's been at our house lately.

Have a peek inside, and you'll see what I mean.

Oops, ignore all that gory stuff I scribbled on the front cover. That curse doesn't apply to our trustworthy Sleepover fans. What? No, of *course* you won't die a horrible agonising death if you read it! I mean, I formally *invited* you to peek, didn't I? OK, if it makes you feel better, I'll cross my heart!! Anyway, here's yesterday's entry:

In just a few hours, it'll be my mum's wedding day. Forget butterflies – I think I've got giant rhinos rampaging in my tummy. I'm really tired but there's no way I'm going to get a WINK of sleep! Until recently I thought weddings were like, mega-happy family events. But if you ask me, they just bring out the worst in everyone. Practically everything that could go wrong with this one has. And the worst thing was – it was ALL my fault! I should never have—

Oh-oh, Amber's whingeing at me to turn out the light, so she can get her beauty sleep. 'Bye for now!

Heh heh heh! I bet that got you going. Now you're going crazy, wondering who on earth the mysterious Amber is, aren't you? Which is excellent news, because I'm DYING to tell you. In fact, if I don't tell someone the whole amazing story pretty soon, I'll probably EXPLODE!

I wasn't exaggerating in my Wedding Diary, by the way. A few days back, my whole life went totally haywire. And I don't want to worry you or anything, but at one point, things got so bad that the fate of the entire Sleepover Club *trembled* in the balance...

9

Are you shocked? Then just imagine how *we* felt!

So hang on for your life, lovely reader, because we're going on a bumpy rollercoaster ride back in time, to the day when my mum's wonderful wedding began to go HORRIBLY pear-shaped...

CHAPTER TWO

Wouldn't it be great if life was like films? Just imagine if you woke up each morning to your very own movie soundtrack! Then, the minute you heard those creepy *durn durn DURN* chords, you'd instantly know to avoid the very bad thing which was lying in wait for you around the corner.

As it was, one of the worst days of my life came without warning.

Actually, it started out great. The sun shone. Mum and Andy giggled over breakfast like two love-birds. I didn't think it was possible for my wildly happy mum and soon-to-be-official step-dad to get any happier, but they were practically GLOWING! And my little brother was in such a sweet mood that he presented me with a truly bizarre drawing.

"Ooh, that's erm, *lovely*, Callum," I said cautiously. I had no idea why Callum had given me a drawing of five orange space aliens, but like Mum says, it's the thought that counts.

"That's you and that's Kenny," he said proudly. "There's Frankie and that's Rosie and Lyndz. You're all wearing your bridesmaids' frocks, look!"

"And what's that?" I asked, pointing at a green figure lurking in the corner of the page.

"Oh, that's a dinosaur out to kill you all," Callum said airily.

Well, he IS seven! But when I bluetacked his drawing to our fridge alongside his other masterpieces, Callum looked really hurt.

"Don't you want to show my brilliant drawing to your friends, Fliss?"

"Oh, silly ole me, what was I thinking of," I said, and I stuffed it into my school bag instead.

I showed it to the others before we went into school, and not surprisingly they fell about.

"Which one's me again?" asked Kenny.

"Isn't it obvious? The one with three eyes," giggled Lyndz.

"Duh," said Rosie. "Anyone can see that's not an eye, it's a nose."

Kenny looked uneasy. "We're not really going to wear dayglo orange dresses, Fliss, are we?"

Honestly, that girl is *so* impossible! She can describe just about every goal scored by Leicester City football team ever since there's BEEN a Leicester City football team, but when it comes to style, she hasn't got a *clue*!

"No, we are NOT wearing dayglo orange," I said patiently. "I've told you about a billion times. We're wearing this really pretty shade of *peach*, OK? Orange was just the closest colour Callum could find in his crayon box."

Kenny pulled a face. "I can't believe you're putting us through this, Fliss," she moaned.

13

"We're going to look totally stoo-pid. Like a bunch of icky *meringues,* or something."

But Kenny didn't fool anybody. She'd never admit it, but Miss Cool 'n' Sporty was every bit as keyed-up about Mum's wedding as the rest of us.

Frankie had gone misty-eyed. "Just think," she breathed. "One day Izzy will be doing cute little drawings for *me*!"

Frankie's baby sister must be about six months old now, but Frankie's still totally mushy about her.

Rosie gave me a nudge. "Fliss, quick! Check out the M&Ms!"

Now there's two girls who should *definitely* come with a warning soundtrack. In case you've forgotten, Emma Hughes and Emily Berryman are the Sleepover Club's deadliest enemies. They're also completely two-faced, which is why grown-ups never believe us when we tell them how mean the M&Ms are. In fact, like Kenny says, most grown-ups think the sun shines out of the M&Ms' you-know-whats!!

I sneaked a look over my shoulder, in time

to catch Emma and Emily madly pretending they weren't eavesdropping on our conversation. You should have seen their faces. They looked exactly like they'd been sucking lemons! The M&Ms can't *stand* anyone else being the centre of attention.

"Heh heh heh," chortled Lyndz. "They must have heard about your mum's wedding. One-nil to you, Flissy."

I've got to admit, it gave me a definite boost, seeing my ten minutes of bridesmaid fame get under our enemies' skins like that. You know, sometimes I think us Sleepover Club girls must be telepathic, because we didn't have to say a single word! We just stalked past the M&Ms, as if we were wearing our long floaty dresses and flowery crowns already!

For the rest of that day, whenever the M&Ms were in earshot, we kept up a non-stop gush of bridesmaid talk. And that's where everything started to go wrong. I'm so sure of this, that if I was making a film of my life, that is *definitely* the part where I'd put in some doomy *durn durn DURN* chords.

You see, the M&Ms are our sworn enemies for one very good reason.

They are NOT nice people, OK?

By the end of the day, we'd managed to get so far up their noses that those girls were practically spitting with envy. If we'd had any sense, we'd have let it go at that. Instead, we decided to carry on flaunting our bridesmaid superstar status to the max.

For obvious reasons, we usually avoid walking home the same way as the M&Ms. But today we trailed them so closely, we were practically walking in their shoes!! We all knew we were playing with fire really, but we were having such a great laugh, we didn't care.

We skipped along arm in arm, swanking loudly about how we were going back to my house for a dress fitting, and how our dresses were totally lush and how Mum and Andy's wedding was going to be at this mega-posh country house.

Then all of a sudden, the M&Ms darted across to the other side of the street, giggling like idiots. And at the same moment Frankie flashed me a worried look. The kind that says "uh-oh."

And there it was, blocking our path. An absolutely MASSIVE ladder.

I don't think the bloke was much of a decorator, because there were paint drips everywhere. I could hear the ladder creaking and swaying like a ship in a storm, as the painter sloshed white gloss on the gutterings and anything else within splattering distance.

The others have probably told you that I'm really superstitious. *Everyone* knows this. So you won't be surprised to hear that walking under ladders is not normally my idea of a fun time. And so this was definitely a *durn durn DURN* moment.

I stopped dead a few metres from the ladder and swallowed hard. I could hear the Gruesome Twosome whispering on the other side of the street, and I just KNEW they were cooking something up.

Suddenly Emily squawked:

"I dare you to walk under that ladder, Felicity Sidebotham!"

"Yeah, right," jeered Emma. "And pigs might fly!"

And from the way the M&Ms smirked, you could tell they thought they'd totally trapped me.

I can't explain what got into me then. It's not like I've ever been the daredevil type. It's true that I was on a serious wedding high, but it was more than that. Maybe I was just fed up with people calling me a wimp all the time.

I gave the M&Ms my iciest stare. "OK," I snapped. "Then you'd better start looking up and checking for flying pig poo!"

The others gasped and Frankie actually made a grab for me, but they were all much too late.

I sailed under that ladder, as smooth as butterscotch. I didn't even cross my fingers inside my pockets. In fact I moved so fast, the others had to put on a real spurt to catch up.

No-one spoke after that. We just kind of marched along in deadly silence. The others looked a bit stunned. The M&Ms had totally vanished. I suppose they'd slithered off to their coffins, or whatever the undead normally do after school.

Finally Frankie said, "Personally, Fliss, I wouldn't have done that. Not *this* week."

"Me neither," said Rosie in an awed voice.

Kenny shook her head. "What got into you, Fliss?"

Lyndz had turned deadly pale. "If that was me, I'd have been wetting myself in case I jinxed the entire wedding."

"Yeah," agreed Frankie. "Walking under ladders pretty much *guarantees* seven days' bad luck. Everyone knows that."

"Rubbish," I said uneasily.

Lyndz practically wrung her hands. "But it's true," she said.

Rosie had been counting on her fingers. "Seven days," she squeaked. "But that takes you right up to the eve of the actual wedding! I mean, Fliss, *anything* could happen. Your house could be struck by a meteorite or something!"

Rosie's words went through me like a knife. And suddenly I totally went to pieces.

19

"Why didn't you guys stop me?" I wailed. "I don't want Mum and Andy to have bad luck. I want everything to go BRILLIANTLY for them!" I covered my face. "I can't *believe* it. I just hexed my mother's future happiness!!"

Usually when I start one of my major doom monologues, the others say sensible things like, "Don't be stoo-pid, Fliss. Have a Cheesy Wotsit and look on the bright side."

But this time, I couldn't help noticing that no-one exactly rushed to contradict me. In fact, no-one said a WORD.

I looked up in a panic, and saw four worried faces staring back at me. This was terrible. All my friends thought I'd ruined Mum's wedding too!!

That DID it. I had the howling heebie jeebies right there in the middle of the street. "I'm such a bad person! I ruin *everything*. I should never have been born!"

The others didn't know what to do. They made sympathetic noises and someone patted me once or twice, but I was in such a state it didn't register. At least, not until Kenny suddenly whacked me really hard.

"Will you shut up!" she yelled. "I'm going to tell you how to cancel the bad luck, OK?" And she fished a clean tissue out of her pocket and handed it over.

I stopped yelling immediately. "Really?" I quavered. I gave my nose a big comforting blow. Then I gazed at Kenny like a hopeful puppy, while she told me what I had to do.

I have no idea where that girl picked up her wedding know-how, but I bet it wasn't at Leicester City football club! I was impressed. I mean, *I'm* the girly superstitious one, right?

Apparently, all I had to do was find four mysterious "somethings" by the actual wedding day and give them to Mum, and the jinx would be like, cancelled!

"Find four what?" frowned Rosie. "Speak English, Kenny."

Kenny sighed and gabbled a quaint little rhyme that went: "Something old, something new, something borrowed, something blue."

"Oh, *those* somethings," the rest of us said immediately.

I wiped my eyes. "I didn't know that was like a good *luck* thing," I sniffled.

21

Lyndz wasn't too impressed. "Fliss's mum seems like the mega-organised type to me," she objected. "She probably had her somethings sorted ages ago."

I gave my nose another big blow. "Uh-uh," I said. "She's been too busy organising all the dresses and the reception and everything to even *think* about good luck stuff."

"Well, there you go," said Kenny smugly. "Now you can take care of them *for* her. That way you get to be a good daughter AND cancel the wicked M&Ms' ladder spell all in one go."

"Yippee!" grinned Rosie. "Now let's go and try on our meringues – I mean, dresses!"

"You'd better not call them that in front of my mum," I warned, cheering up a bit more.

Mum was making our bridesmaid dresses herself. I helped pick out the colour, actually. It was also my idea to have like, cute little ballet shoes dyed to match. Mum had gone to loads of trouble, sitting up night after night, stitching away, and now the dresses were almost ready. The fitting was just for Mum to check the hems before she finished them on her machine.

Actually, I think Mum was as excited about the dresses as we were, because she whipped open the door before I could even get my key out.

"Do you girls fancy a little snack," she said, "before we do the fitting?"

Frankie giggled. "Maybe we should have the fitting and *then* have our little snack," she said. (I don't know if the others have told you, but my mum's snacks are sometimes a wee bit over the top and take *forever* to prepare!)

"Good point," agreed Kenny.

"Oh, well, if you're sure." Mum flew upstairs to fetch the dresses. She called down to us from the landing: "Shut your eyes, girls!"

"Mu-um!" I moaned. "We're not five years old."

We shut our eyes all the same. There was loads of mysterious rustling as Mum came back downstairs. Suddenly I got this wildly excited feeling, like you do just before you open your eyes on Christmas morning.

"You can look now," said Mum, sounding breathless.

She had draped the dresses over the sofa, so we could see them properly. We gasped.

"Oh, they are so-o *gorgeous*," breathed Rosie.

The last time I'd seen the fabric, Mum was struggling to cut out gazillions of fiddly little pattern pieces on our living-room floor. So I was every bit as dazzled as the others.

"We're going to look like fairy-tale princesses," whispered Lyndz.

"Some of us, maybe," muttered Kenny. "The rest of us will look like total—"

"You first, Kenny dear," said Mum brightly.

Good ole Kenny! We could tell she was absolutely freaking out inside, but she stood there like a docile little lamb and let Mum slip her rustly satin dress over her head. Though it was just as well Mum was concentrating on Kenny's hemline, because Kenny's *face* was a total picture.

The minute Mum disappeared to hunt for a tape measure, Kenny clenched her fists. "Don't any of you say a WORD," she hissed.

"I KNEW I'd look like a meringue."

Frankie frowned. "Actually," she said, "you look really pretty."

"*Pretty!*" Kenny snarled. "Huh! Don't make me laugh!"

Honestly, I wish you could have seen that girl, pulling hideous troll faces at us in her frothy peachy bridesmaid's dress. We all cracked up.

Naturally, Kenny thought we were laughing because she looked awful in the dress. She clawed at it furiously, trying to get it off, but Mum had pinned the material at the back, so she was basically trapped.

Luckily, just then Mum walked back in and said a totally perfect thing.

"Oh, Kenny," she said softly. "You make that dress look so special."

We could see Kenny struggling to figure out if "special" was some kind of polite adult code for "weird". Then she gave my mum a shy little grin.

"Hey, thanks Mrs Sidebotham," she said. "Erm – about that snack?"

CHAPTER THREE

Did I tell you we'd planned to hold our next sleepover the following Saturday? In other words, immediately AFTER the wedding?

Don't laugh, but for some reason I felt completely unhinged every time I heard myself say those three little words.

After the wedding. After the wedding. After the...

It was like I couldn't imagine it. As if the wedding was making HUGE quantities of fog, and I couldn't see anything beyond it.

I'd known about Mum and Andy getting married since New Year, yet I still couldn't quite believe it was going to happen. I think Mum felt that way too. She'd been really stressed out the last few days. In fact, on Friday night she went to bed practically the same time I did!

When I woke up on Saturday morning I snuggled under my duvet, picturing how thrilled Mum would be with me for tracking down her lucky somethings all by myself. Obviously I didn't plan to spoil my good deed by mentioning the evil ladder spell. Besides, if Kenny was right, that stupid ladder didn't have a chance against my four magical gifts.

I chanted the rhyme softly under my quilt. "Something old, something new, something borrowed, something blue."

Suddenly I sat up, totally freaked out. *Yikes!* I had exactly one week left to get my act together!! Not to mention that I still hadn't figured out what my brother and I were giving Mum and Andy for a wedding present...

"Oh well," I sighed. "I've got all today to crack that one."

But as it turned out, I was totally wrong about this.

When I went downstairs, Mum and Andy were rushing round like maniacs, cleaning the house.

"What's up, you two? Is the Queen Mum dropping by?" I joked.

My mother gave me a funny look, scurried off with the vacuum cleaner and started blasting the hall with Shake 'n Vac.

Andy looked surprised. "Didn't Nikky tell you my mother's coming to stay?" he said.

"Uh-uh," I said.

"She probably forgot," said Andy. He lowered his voice. "It's not surprising. Your mum's got a lot on her mind."

"Tell me about it," I sighed. I filled a bowl with my favourite strawberry cereal and joined Callum in front of *Live & Kicking*.

"Hey, shorty!" I hissed. "What can I get Mum that's like, *old*? Oh, I also need something blue?"

My brother frowned. "Andy's got some stinky old cheese in the fridge," he suggested. "That's quite blue." He suddenly remembered something. "You probably shouldn't give it to Mum though. I heard her tell Andy to put it in the bin. She said it made her want to throw up, *big* time."

I sighed. Looks like you're on your own with this one Fliss, I told myself.

Andy popped his head round the door. "I'm just going to fetch my mum from the station. Anyone want to come?"

"ME ME ME!" yelled Callum, jumping up and down.

"How about you, Fliss?" Andy asked.

I pointed to my pink baby doll pyjamas. "I don't *think* so, Andy," I giggled.

Mum came scurrying back with the vacuum cleaner. She stared at me. "Why aren't you dressed?"

"Duh! It's Saturday," I said. Then I saw what she was doing. "Mum, are you nuts? You vacuumed in here three minutes ago."

Mum seemed amazed. "Are you sure?"

"Totally."

Mum giggled. "Oops," she said. "Look, Fliss, get a move on, there's a love. Patsy will be here in half an hour." She looked as if the very idea of meeting her future mother-in-law made her want to faint.

"I'm going, I'm going," I grumbled. "You're not the only person with stuff to do, you know," I added mysteriously.

Personally I thought Patsy was an incredibly sad name for an adult, but apart from that, I was looking forward to meeting Andy's mum. Maybe she could help me out with my four somethings. Plus, she'd probably bring us cool presents. After all, she was *kind* of our grandma.

Andy never talked much about his family. But it was obvious he totally worshipped his mum. Andy's dad died when Andy was really little, so his mum brought him up by herself.

After my shower, I tried on practically everything in my wardrobe. In the end I decided to put on this new summer dress Mum got me in Leicester. I expect you can guess what colour it was!

Actually this particular dress is a really *delicious* pink, that delicate sugar-mouse colour which looks really perfect with blonde hair. Then I brushed my hair and fastened it back with some sweet little slides.

"Why haven't we met Patsy before?" I asked, as Mum and I waited for everyone to arrive. "I mean, you and Andy have been together for AGES."

But at that moment Mum vanished rather suddenly into the downstairs loo, so I never heard the answer to my question.

By the time she came out again, Andy's car was pulling up outside. Then his mum got out (*Durn durn DURN!*) and I figured it out for myself in ten seconds flat.

I'd have probably figured it out sooner, but I was distracted by Patsy's clothes at first. They were *gorgeous* – well, you know, for an old person. But then I got a good look at Patsy herself, and my heart sank.

You know how some people have naturally friendly faces? Well, Patsy Proudlove has a naturally UNfriendly face.

Mum rushed out and gave her a big hug. Patsy forced a smile, but you could see hugging wasn't her favourite activity.

"And this is Fliss," said Mum brightly.

"So I see," said Patsy, as if she'd been

spying on me by satellite and wasn't too impressed.

"We've all been dying to meet you, Patsy," said Mum.

Then we all stood around like a game of statues, and it was glaringly obvious that no-one could think of ANYTHING to say!

Andy rubbed his hands together, something I never *ever* saw him do before. "Well, isn't this, er – great!" he beamed. "Shall we go into the living room, and catch up with everyone's news?"

"I'd rather see my room first, if you don't mind, dear," said Patsy in a brisk voice. "And perhaps someone would show me where I can wash my hands. You wouldn't believe the state of those trains." And she said it as if the state of Britain's trains was *our* fault!

Andy carried Patsy's stuff up to the spare room. Patsy followed stiffly in her gorgeous clothes.

What's *her* problem, I thought.

Without looking at me, Mum crossed the hall and moved a harmless little vase for absolutely no reason. "Erm, did you put out those guest towels like I asked you?" she said. She sounded really uptight.

I was getting that churning feeling. The one I get when Mum's stressing about something and I don't know what to do about it.

"Mum," I whispered. "Is Patsy going to be staying here all *week*? You know, until the wedding?"

Mum looked shocked. "Where else would she stay? She *is* Andy's mother. It's really good of her to offer to lend us a hand."

"Mmn," I said in a neutral kind of voice. But what I was thinking was EEK! I'd rather win a night out with Darth Maul!!

Anyway, I won't go into too many lurid details about our first day with Andy's mum. All you need to know is that it was deeply depressing.

Patsy was the kind of person who has strong views on everything. Pop music, TV soaps, dog poo, you name it. And once she got started she just kept on and on, battering away at Mum like a bulldozer. And Mum just sat there, smiling bravely, and totally letting herself be bulldozed!

I kept expecting Andy to tell his mum where to get off, but it was like he didn't even *notice*! And all at once these scary new thoughts came slithering into my mind like poisonous snakes. Like, what if Andy didn't really love us after all?

I felt like I was seeing a totally different side of my almost-step-dad. I got the definite feeling that if you asked Andy to choose between us and his sour-puss mother, he'd root for her every time.

After lunch, I escaped into the kitchen to make tea for everyone. And can you believe Patsy had the *nerve* to follow me!

"No, no dear," she said impatiently. "You've put enough water in that kettle to sink the Titanic. Do you think your stepfather's made of money?"

That was the last straw. And the minute Patsy left the kitchen, I made a sneaky phone call to Rosie.

"Can I come over?" I hissed. "It's an emergency."

"Sure," she said. "I'll tell the others."

I popped my head round the living-room door. "Erm, I've just remembered I was meant to meet up with my friends today," I fibbed. "I won't be long. See you later everyone." Then I grabbed my jacket and slammed out of the house.

I stormed along, getting to Rosie's house in record time.

Luckily Rosie let me in and we went straight up to her room, so I didn't even have to be polite to her mum or anything.

I paced up and down Rosie's bedroom until the others turned up, and then I just splurted out the whole story.

"Since I walked under that ladder, everything's fallen apart," I ranted. "Mum's gone totally wobbly. Andy's mother is this like, nightmare person! And Andy's not even *trying* to stop her."

Kenny rolled her eyes. "I already told you how to cancel the ladder spell. You were meant to get cracking on those somethings today."

"How could I? I haven't had a minute to

myself," I fumed. "How was I supposed to know Patsy Proudlove was coming? No-one ever tells me *anything*!"

Lyndz grinned. "You make Andy's Mum sound like one of those huge thingummies!"

We stared at her.

"You know," she said. "The things that flatten towns and stir up tidal waves."

"What, like a hurricane?" asked Kenny.

Lyndz nodded, her eyes glinting wickedly. The others cracked up.

"Yikes! Hurricane Patsy's coming. Everyone down into the cellar!" cackled Frankie.

But I couldn't even raise a smile. "It's so unfair," I moaned. "She's spoiling everything. And Mum's just letting her." I slumped to the floor. "And I STILL don't know what to get them for a wedding present."

"Well, we can't do much about Hurricane Patsy, but we could give you some prezzie ideas," suggested Rosie. "That might take some of the pressure off."

"Thanks, Rosie Posie," I croaked. "That would be great."

Rosie tore some pages out of a notebook and handed them round, along with various-sized bits of pencil.

"The thing is, it's got to be really unusual," I explained. "But it can't cost too much. And it can't be something they've got already."

Honestly, my friends are so sweet! They came up with masses of things, from parrots to peg bags. Actually, I was really into the parrot idea until Kenny pointed out that they cost thousands of pounds.

"Plus they poo everywhere from a great height," giggled Lyndz. "I don't think Fliss's mum would be too happy about that."

"It was just an *idea*," said Frankie huffily. "Fliss *said* she wanted something unusual."

"Parrot poo is unusual all right," spluttered Lyndz.

And you can guess what happened then, can't you? Yep, Lyndz had one of her famous hiccup attacks.

By the time she'd recovered, I wasn't just confused. I also felt guilty. My friends were knocking themselves out trying to cheer me up. So why was I still so depressed?

Finally we all went downstairs and Rosie made us drinks. She wanted us to try her new craze – something called a smoothy. Basically, you put fruit and natural yoghurt in the blender and whizz it till it's (surprise surprise) SMOOTH!

This time, Rosie whizzed raspberries, bananas and mango with yoghurt, and it was totally velvety and delicious.

"Know what I wish?" I said suddenly. "I wish this whole stupid wedding business was over. Then everything could just go back to how it was."

Frankie sighed. "Dream on, Flissy," she said. "Because that's never going to happen. I mean, when it's over Andy's going to be your *official* step-dad. That's *big*!"

The others nodded. Kenny looked serious. "Everything's going to change, Fliss," she said. "Everything."

After I switched off my lamp that night, Kenny's words came back to me. *Everything's going to change. Everything.*

"What if it's a bad change?" I whispered to myself. "What if this whole wedding idea is a big mistake, and none of us is ever happy again?" And I had a scared little sniffle into my pillow.

Just as I was finally dozing off, the phone rang downstairs. Who on earth could it be? It was practically midnight!

Andy took the call, then yelled for Mum. Then next minute Mum totally screamed her head off. My heart started to race. Something terrible must have happened. I jumped out of bed and ran downstairs.

"Mum! Mum! What's wrong?"

Mum waved at me to keep quiet. "You're actually here at Heathrow!" she shrieked into the phone, beaming all over her face. "So how come you kept me in the dark all this time? Oh, it's a surprise all right! Oh, Jilly, you've completely made my day. Wait till I tell Fliss!"

I sat on the stairs with a bump. Jilly lived in the United States. She was Mum's oldest and most unpredictable friend. Mum had been really disappointed when Jilly wrote to say she couldn't make it to the wedding. And now she'd turned up in the UK, just like that!

"Wait till you tell Fliss what?" I asked as Mum put down the phone.

Mum grabbed me and twirled me round. "Jilly's daughter came over with her. Isn't that great? You two are almost exactly the same age. Oh, Flissy, you two are going to have such fun, just like Jilly and I used to. And you're going to meet her tomorrow!"

I went back to bed in a happy daze. Jilly doesn't just live in the USA. She actually lives in *Los Angeles*, where the film stars hang out. That practically made Jilly and her daughter film stars too.

I stretched out under my quilt, and grinned to myself in the dark. I was going to be best friends with a film star! I could hardly believe my luck!

It's going to be all right, I thought. Everything is going to be ALL RIGHT.

Suddenly I was so happy that even though Andy's mum was in the next room, rattling the wardrobe with her juicy snores, I didn't give a hoot!

CHAPTER FOUR

Next morning, I rushed downstairs, dying to tell the others my news. But the instant I picked up the phone, Mum flew out of the kitchen, hissing like an angry swan. "SSSH! You'll wake Patsy. She'll be wanting a nice Sunday lie-in!"

"Fat chance in this house," grinned Andy.

But as it turned out, all this tiptoeing around was a total waste of time. About half an hour later, Andy took his mum up a cup of tea and found her sitting on the edge of her bed in her Sunday best, waiting for us to tell her it was OK to come down!

Patsy didn't actually say, but it was obvious this was a major black mark against Mum for not making her feel more welcome.

"I'm sure I don't want to get in anyone's way," she sniffed, as she poured herself a bowl of branflakes.

I sidled up to Andy. "Now can I use the phone?" I whispered.

Patsy overheard. "Use the PHONE!" she said, horrified. "She's just a child! She might ring Australia by mistake!"

"Oh, Fliss wouldn't do anything like that," said Mum quickly. "She's far too sensible."

I thought Mum still looked horribly pale. This wedding business is wearing her out, I thought.

"Thanks, Mum, you're a star," I whispered in her ear as I went past. And I grabbed the phone and escaped upstairs to my room.

"ANOTHER emergency?" said Rosie disbelievingly. "That's TWO, in twenty-four hours!"

"Yeah, but this one is a *cool* emergency," I said.

"OK!" she sighed. "See ya."

An hour later, we all piled into Frankie's pad. Frankie's mum had given everyone home-made slush puppies, plus a stash of kitchen towel to mop up the drips. Everyone made themselves comfy on Frankie's silver floor cushions. That girl goes for silver in a BIG way!

"Go on, Fliss, give!" beamed Rosie.

"Yeah, we want all the goss about Jilly's daughter," said Lyndz.

I felt myself go bright red. I don't know why I blush so easily, but I really wish I didn't! "What do you want to know?" I said.

"Everything," said Frankie at once.

"Well, she's about our age and her name is Amber Glass," I began.

"That's such a cool name!" cried Lyndz.

"And apparently, she's amazingly pretty."

"Like that actually matters," growled Kenny.

"Did I say it mattered?" I snapped. "I'm just describing Amber, OK!"

"Ignore her, Fliss," said Frankie. "So what's she like?"

"She's meant to be incredibly talented," I

43

said. "She's on TV, like all the time. She's got an agent and everything."

Lyndz's eyes almost popped out of her head. "She's ten years old and she's a film star already!"

"Well, *practically*," I said. "She's done loads of commercials anyway."

"Wow," said Rosie. "A wedding and a Hollywood celebrity in the same week!"

"I want Amber to have a really good time while she's here," I said. "It'd be great if you guys could help out."

"Count me in," said Rosie at once.

Lyndz hugged herself. "Can't wait!" she said gleefully.

"I wish it was the holidays already," sighed Frankie. "We could take her to Alton Towers."

"Get real," objected Kenny. "You're talking about a girl who can pop into Disney World any time she likes."

Even Frankie agreed there wasn't much point trying to impress a girl who had her own mobile phone.

"Let's face it, Cuddington's not exactly

LA," I sighed.

Frankie did a cheesey double take. "Yikes! So *that's* why there's never any high-speed car chases round here!"

Kenny threw a pillow at her. "We're trying to think, Frankie!"

"We could go to Bradgate Park after school," suggested Lyndz. "We could have a picnic and check out the cute little baby deer."

"Excellent! We can show her Lady Jane Grey's house," gushed Frankie. "My dad says Americans *lurve* history!"

Bradgate Park is meant to be this major local beauty spot. I probably liked it when I was little, but now I think it's got WAY too much fresh air. I always come back with earache.

"Why would Amber want to see a load of old ruins?" I said. "I mean, it's not like Lady Jane's going to invite us in for strawberries and cream."

"But it's so romantic," Frankie gushed. "I mean Lady Jane was like a child *queen*. And all those—"

"Romantic! You're joking. The poor kid got her head chopped off!" Kenny's eyes gleamed. "And did you know, they hardly *ever* did it with one swing! Sometimes they had to hack away at their—"

"*Kenny*," pleaded Lyndz. "I'm eating a raspberry slush puppy here."

"Yeah, Kenny," glared Frankie. "Plus I hadn't actually finished what I was saying, which was, erm – that all those deer in Bradgate Park today are descended from the deer which Lady Jane Grey herself may actually have—"

"—eaten," Kenny grinned.

Frankie scowled. "You have to make fun of everything."

"Why don't we just do exactly what we always do?" said Rosie. "That way it will be a change for Amber. Plus we'll have a good time."

Everyone thought this was excellent advice. There was a short pause. Then Lyndz coughed. "Let me just get this straight. We're talking typical fun-type activities to share with Amber, is that right?"

"Right," said everyone.

"The usual wacky stuff we do?"

"Totally," we agreed,

There was another, longer pause.

"Any ideas?" I asked finally.

Kenny tapped the side of her head. "Nope. Total blank."

"Blankety blank," Lyndz agreed.

"Ditto," said Rosie.

Frankie tugged her hair. "This is so *stoo-pid*," she complained. "I mean, the five of us have SO much fun, like *constantly*."

"Constantly," Rosie echoed.

"Oh, absolutely," agreed Kenny, totally straight-faced. "In fact, I'm not sure I can take any more excitement."

Frankie's lips twitched. "You are such a pig, Kenny," she giggled. And suddenly we all cracked up laughing.

"Let's wait till Amber gets here," said Lyndz sensibly. "She's the guest. We'll ask her what she wants to do."

So after that, we just hung around at Frankie's house, enjoyably messing about, till it was time for everybody's dinner.

But as I turned into our street, I remembered something. I'd promised myself to come up with my Something Blue today. Also, I still hadn't a CLUE what to get Mum and Andy for a wedding present. Then my tummy gave a big rumble. Oh, well, I'll think about it after dinner, I thought greedily.

Sunday dinner is like, this major production in our house. Six days a week, Mum is incredibly diet-conscious. But on Sundays she totally goes to town. Just thinking about Mum's roast chicken, with all the yummy trimmings, made my mouth water. Mmmn, I couldn't wait!

I let myself in through our front door, getting ready to breathe in that special Sunday dinner aroma. Then...

What in the WORLD is that gruesome pong? I thought.

It smelled *exactly* like bad drains!! I flew into the kitchen, to warn my parents they had a major plumbing problem on their hands. But for some reason, our kitchen was completely deserted. Normally at this stage on a Sunday, Mum is whizzing about like a celebrity chef on *Ready Steady Cook*, draining veggies and crisping up the roast spuds.

Then I noticed a Bad Sign. (*Durn durn durn!!*)

Instead of three or four pans cheerfully steaming away on the hob, there was one MASSIVE pan, glooping and glopping like a witch's cauldron. I had accidentally located the source of the bad-drain smell.

The saucepan was getting alarmingly hyperactive, as its contents tried to escape from under the lid. Suddenly, green slime began to dribble over the sides.

Andy's mum bustled in. "So you're back, finally," she snapped. "Just as well. Dinner's practically ready."

"Erm, so where is it?" I said. I wasn't trying to be funny. It truly never occurred to me that my Sunday dinner could resemble the experiment of an evil scientist.

"I took over the cooking. Your mother needs a rest. She's worn out," Patsy sighed. She made it sound like my fault – as if I was some selfish vampire child, draining my mother's blood supply.

"But we *always* have a roast on Sundays," I wailed.

Patsy snorted. "The traditional Sunday roast is a waste of time and energy. Takes all morning, wrecks the entire kitchen, and in five minutes it's forgotten. My soup takes twenty minutes and requires one pan. Far more sensible, don't you think?" She gave a grim smile.

I stared queasily at the overflowing pan. "That's *soup*?"

"I knew your mother was diet-conscious, what with the wedding coming up. Cabbage soup is *perfect* for slimmers. Maybe you've heard of the Cabbage Soup diet?"

"Er no," I said, truthfully.

Patsy lifted the saucepan lid and sniffed rapturously. "I'll just add the finishing touches," she said.

Yeah, like stir in some scrummy cat-sick, I thought. And I rushed off to plead with my parents.

Andy seemed more interested in the

motor-racing than listening to me. He didn't even take his eyes off the screen. "Patsy's just being helpful," he mumbled.

"It won't hurt just this once, Fliss," said Mum. She dropped her voice. "Just have a couple of spoonfuls to be polite. There's chocolate fudge brownies for dessert. I thought we'd all have a little pre-wedding treat!"

A high-pitched whine came from the kitchen as Andy's mum operated our liquidiser at high speed.

I swallowed bravely. "I suppose," I said.

In a few minutes we were all sitting round the table. Patsy brought the pan to the table, still sputtering furiously. (The pan, not Patsy, you nutcase!)

Unfortunately, its trip through the liquidiser hadn't exactly improved Patsy's soup. Now it looked like those bubbling mud springs you see on documentaries.

My brother looked panic-stricken. "I can't eat that," he whispered. "It's still alive."

I wanted to giggle, but the soup smelled so terrible I was scared to breathe.

"Try some, Callum. It'll put hairs on your chest," said Andy in a jokey voice I'd never heard him use before today.

Callum blew on a spoonful of sludge, shut his eyes and downed it in one. "Ouf!" he shuddered.

"Well?" said Patsy stiffly. "What do you think?"

"Ooh, that's really yummy, isn't it, Callum?" Mum hinted.

My little brother stared wildly around the table. I could practically see his thought bubbles. Help! What do I do? Fibbing is bad. Being rude is also very bad.

Then his face suddenly cleared, as he came up with the perfect reply. "I'll tell you one thing," he said cheerfully. "It's not *nearly* as bad as it looks!"

"*Callum!*" said Mum.

"Well, REALLY!" huffed Patsy.

But I thought my little brother was a total star. I was pretty heroic myself. I actually forced down one whole spoonful. But once my throat knew what was coming, it went on strike, refusing to let any more khaki gloop near my stomach. So I just kept my spoon busy, to give the impression I was slurping away like Oliver Twist.

Even nightmares have to end, I told myself. Soon I'd be tucking into one of Mum's highly calorific chocolate brownies. I'd never been too crazy about brownies in the past, but now that Amber was coming, all things American seemed incredibly groovy! Not to mention the fact that I was STARVING!!

All through dinner, Patsy was getting more and more tight-lipped. Suddenly she started collecting up the soup bowls, rattling the crockery like you would not *believe*.

"Well!" she sniffed. "We all know what happens to boys and girls who don't eat their dinner, don't we?"

Everyone stared at her. Even Mum and Andy looked startled.

Patsy drew herself up to her full height. "NO PUDDING!" she thundered. And she flounced out to the kitchen.

Callum's face fell a million miles.

"She can't do that!" I said in horror. "Tell her, Andy! Tell her, Mum!"

But Mum and Andy didn't say a word.

"You're not going to let her get away with it?" I pleaded.

Andy cleared his throat. "Don't make a big deal out of this, OK."

"Big deal?!" I yelled. "Do you know what I've had to eat today? A piece of toast and a raspberry slush puppy, that's what!"

"Fliss, please," murmured Mum. "You'll hurt Patsy's feelings."

That was the last straw.

"*Patsy*'s feelings?" I screamed. "What about *MINE*?"

I stormed upstairs to my room and slammed the door.

I wasn't just angry. I was scared. What was going on? Overnight my parents had somehow turned into these weird strangers. I felt as if I'd walked into one of those sc-fi films, where no-one is what they seem, and the evil bodysnatchers are in town. If my parents were going to carry on like this, they didn't DESERVE a wedding present!!

I picked up my giant pink teddy bear and gave him a major cuddle.

Before I knew it, I'd drifted off into a deeply satisfying daydream, where Mum's friend Jilly and her daughter liked me so much that they insisted on taking me back with them to Hollywood, where they fed me all the chocolate fudge brownies I could eat...

CHAPTER FIVE

The minute I got into the school playground, I dashed up to the others and started pouring out my tragic story.

I was just describing my cabbage soup ordeal in heartrending detail, when Kenny started biting her lip. Then I noticed Frankie was madly stuffing her fingers in her mouth. And suddenly Lyndz gave this humungous piggy snort.

I couldn't believe it. My friends were LAUGHING!

"I'm glad YOU think it's funny," I said huffily.

"I'm sorry," Rosie gasped. "It sounds awful, Fliss. You must have been so upset."

Of course, that did it. Everyone totally cracked up!

All of a sudden I completely saw the funny side. (Which is most unlike me!) For some reason, all the things which seemed so terrible yesterday struck me as absolutely hysterical today!

By the time I'd got to the part about Mum and Andy being taken over by alien bodysnatchers, we were staggering around the playground, shrieking with laughter.

Honestly, talk about Giggle Therapy! I felt HEAPS better. Plus, my mates helped me put everything into perspective.

"It's not like Hurricane Patsy is going to be staying at your place for ever," Rosie pointed out, as we lined up to go into class.

"And don't worry about your mum and dad," said Frankie sympathetically. "Grown-ups often act weird around their parents."

"Amber's coming, that's the main thing," said Lyndz. "I can't wait! I never met a real film star before."

"Yeah," said Rosie. "It's SO great you don't mind sharing her with us, Fliss!"

"Mum thought we'd all go into Leicester after school tomorrow," I told them. "Want to come?"

And my friends were so obviously thrilled to be invited that I started to feel like a bit of a celebrity myself.

When I got home, I was surprised to find Andy home from work already. He looked so smart I hardly recognised him.

"Oooh!" I teased. "Is this in Jilly's honour? Should Mum be jealous?"

"Er, yeah," Andy said. "That's exactly it, Fliss. I like to keep your Mum on her toes."

I noticed that my laidback step-dad had this really tense expression for some reason. Plus both he and Mum seemed unusually quiet. But I decided they just had butterflies, like me.

I went rushing upstairs to make myself look especially nice for Amber. After I'd had a long hot shower, I put on my new ice-blue jeans, and a sweet little T-shirt with the word ANGEL on it, in really tasteful lettering. I've got this real thing about angels lately, I don't know why. Plus, apparently they're HUGE in America.

I brushed my hair till it was all soft and silky, then I put in my flowery clips.

I checked my reflection nervously in the mirror on my dressing table. And you know what? I'm not being vain or anything, but I thought I looked quite pretty. And for, like fifty seconds, everything felt so perfect that I honestly wouldn't have swapped places with anyone else in the world.

Actually my life was getting more and more like TV! Fifty seconds of pure happiness, then that music goes *durn durn DURN*, and you know everything is going to go drastically downhill...

Well, that's how it was with me.

Last Christmas, Andy gave me this cute hand-mirror. Don't tell the others, but secretly I thought it looked like the kind of thing a mermaid might own. It lived on my dressing table, next to this bottle of really expensive bath stuff which my real dad, Steve, got me.

Anyway, I suddenly thought I'd like to see how my hair clips looked close up, so I went to pick up the mirror.

CRASH!!!

It slipped from my hands, bounced off my dressing table, and smashed into pieces.

I stared at it in total shock. I have no idea how it even happened. The mirror wasn't heavy. And my hands weren't sweaty or anything.

I was still staring at the mess, when Andy's mum rushed in, like a bad fairy in a pantomime. "How could you be so thoughtless, Felicity!" she cried. "That's seven years' bad luck!"

"I didn't break it on purpose!" I wailed. But inside I was turning numb with horror. And I'd thought seven DAYS' bad luck was terrible news!

I realised Patsy had beetled off to tell my parents what I'd done. So I dashed downstairs to tell them my side of the story. But I was too late.

Andy's face was like thunder. "Is this true, Fliss?" he said.

"I don't even know how it happened!" I wailed. "We won't *really* get seven years' bad luck, will we?"

I should explain that normally Andy is the most easy-going guy on this planet. But as you know, these days my family was totally NOT normal.

"How COULD you be so careless?" he yelled. "A great big girl like you!"

Don't you hate it when people call you a "great big girl"? It makes you feel like some hideous troll child. All yesterday's bad feelings came whooshing back. Why was Andy being so mean? Couldn't he see I was miserable about breaking his special present to me?

When I'd found that little gift-wrapped mirror under our Christmas tree last year, I'd felt all warm and fuzzy inside, and I just knew my step-dad really and truly loved me. But right now, I wasn't sure Andy even *liked* me any more. And all at once I burst into floods of tears.

I hate how I look when I cry. I look exactly like those rabbits which those naff conjurors used to pull out of hats. The creepy white kind with pink eyes. (Pink-eyed rabbits, you wally, not pink-eyed conjurors!)

So it was bad luck that Mum's best friend, Jilly, picked that precise moment to lean on our bell, sending the door-chimes into a frenzy of ding-dongs.

"Omigod! It's them!" shrieked Mum. She rushed to the door.

And there on our step were Mum's friend and her famous film-star daughter. I stared at them, totally stunned.

As you probably guessed, it wasn't Jilly who took my breath away. She looked quite sweet and everything, but she was just average mum-material. It was Amber. She was the prettiest girl I've ever seen. Everything about her was gorgeous. Her eyes, her teeth, her hair. Her hair wasn't blonde. It was literally *golden*. As for her clothes, they were out of this world.

I do my best to keep up with the styles (which isn't easy when you live in a dump like Cuddington). But so far as I could see, Amber was in a completely unique style category of her own. She was totally, devastatingly perfect.

Finally Mum and Jilly stopped hugging each other and Mum registered that I was still standing there, lost for words. "Well, say hello to Amber, darling," she said.

Adults can be so tactless. Personally, I'd have thought it was bad enough having perfect Amber see me with my pink-rimmed rabbity eyes, without Mum carrying on like I was some sulky little kid. But there you go.

I scowled. "Give me a chance," I hissed. Nice one, Fliss, I thought immediately. That made you look extremely mature.

Then Amber did something which really showed me up. She stuck out her perfectly manicured hand and gave me a dazzling smile. "Hi," she said. "You must be Fliss. I'm Amber."

"Hi," I mumbled, feeling a real wally.

As you can see, Amber and I hadn't exactly got off to a flying start. But I reassured myself we'd make up for it, as soon we were on our own.

I hung about politely, while Mum and Andy

showed our guests over the house and demonstrated the power shower – you know the kind of thing. And at last Mum said, "Fliss, we won't be eating till quite late. Maybe you could take Amber on a grand tour of Cuddington? You could introduce her to your friends."

I knew this was blatant mother-type code for "We're dying to have a juicy gossip so let's get you girls out of earshot!" But the words were music to my ears.

"Would that be OK with you, Amber?" I asked shyly.

"Sure," said Amber, without enthusiasm. "That would be great."

The minute we got outside, Amber produced a pair of designer sunglasses and perched them on her divine little nose, which only made her look more depressingly perfect than ever.

A wave of panic washed over me. Amber and I were alone together, like I'd wanted. But I still couldn't think of a thing to say.

I mean, plenty of stuff wafted into my mind, but when I imagined actually saying any of it out loud to Amber, it seemed so *babyish* somehow. So there was this squirmingly long silence, and I completely didn't know what to do. Silences don't crop up that often when I'm with my sleepover mates. I mean, Frankie even talks in her sleep!

At last, to break the ice, I blurted, "We're going to Frankie's house. I told the others to meet us there."

Amber made a neutral American "Uhuh" noise and kept on walking.

I was going hot and cold by this time. I had to say *something*!

"I thought Frankie's was the safest bet," I explained. "I'm honestly not being horrible. But you never know *what* state Lyndz's house is going to be in. Her dad's always doing these major renovations. One time they couldn't find the telly for like, days!"

"Really," drawled Amber, making it rhyme with "silly".

"It's just the same at Rosie's," I gushed. "But for a completely different reason. Her mum and dad bought this whacking great

65

house that needed masses doing to it. But then her dad walked out on them. They've done loads of improvements since then, but Rosie still worries that people will think she lives in a real tip."

You really despise me now, don't you? You're thinking, was Fliss out of her fluffy pink mind? Slanging off her best friends to some girl she'd only just met? And I totally don't blame you. All I can say is I TRULY didn't mean to.

I just wanted Amber to know how incredibly, well – *interesting* all my mates were. Only for some reason it came out sounding like they all came from problem families or something!

"We could have gone to Kenny's house, I suppose," I wittered desperately. "But then we'd have had to put up with her sister, Molly, poking her nose in all the time. Also Kenny has this rat."

Amber crinkled her nose. "Ugh," she said faintly. "Shouldn't they put down poison or something?"

I burst into fits of girly giggles. "Oh, I didn't

mean they have, like – RATS. It's a pet. Kenny keeps it in the garage."

"But still," said Amber. "A *rodent*!"

To my relief, I saw that we were nearly at Frankie's house.

"You're going to love Frankie," I gushed. "She's SO much fun. Being with her is just one long party."

You probably won't believe this, but it turned out that my horrendous walk with Amber was actually the *good* part!

As Amber and I went upstairs to Frankie's room, I could hear all my mates merrily slanging off the M&Ms like normal.

"They SO think they're the centre of the universe," Lyndz was saying. And Kenny chortled. "Not!"

Then we opened the door, and everyone looked up, and there was this like, ELECTRIC moment. I could practically see their thought bubbles. "Eeek! What do we say to this perfect person!"

This time Amber showed us *all* up. She stuck out her hand, and said, "Oh, hi!" with that killing American politeness.

I hastily introduced everyone. And Amber looked Rosie right in the eye, and said (eek! it gives me goosebumps just thinking of it!), "So you're Rosie. Gee, that's too bad about your dad."

Rose gave me this murderous look. Luckily, before she could give me a piece of her mind, good ole Frankie went into her Famous Actress routine.

"So Amber," she gushed. "What's it actually *like* living in LA?"

Amber's eyes lit up. "You guys can NOT imagine. It's SO fabulous."

It was like Frankie had turned some magic key. Amber totally sprang to life, telling us about her huge house, the stars she'd met, the parties she went to, the soap she'd just auditioned for – oh yes, and her FABULOUS boyfriend Darryl.

Now and then one of the others opened their mouths to say something, but now Amber had started, she just went on and on. The rest of us just gradually glazed over. Afterwards Kenny said that if Amber had said "fabulous" one more time, she'd have been forced to bang her head on the floor. Her *own* head, Kenny meant. Personally I'd have settled for putting a large paper bag over Amber's.

It's quite funny really. On the way home, things were completely reversed. Amber was still in "fabulous" chat-show mode, and I hardly said a dicky bird!

When we got in, I immediately went in search of Mum. I was in serious need of a girly talk, I can tell you.

I started up the stairs. Andy must have heard me, because he popped his head out of the kitchen. "I wouldn't disturb your mum just yet, Fliss," he said. He had that weird, tense expression I'd noticed earlier, when I was winding him up about coming home especially to see Jilly.

"I can go to the loo, can't I?" I moaned. "Amber's in the other one."

Well it wasn't an actual lie. I did go to the bathroom *first*.

Then I stopped outside Mum's bedroom door and hung about for a couple of seconds. I could hear them talking in whispers. Then I heard these muffled choking sounds.

Someone was *crying*. I think I'm a bit psychic, because right away I just knew that the person doing the crying wasn't Jilly. It was my mum.

I went into a complete panic. I tapped on the door, and without waiting for an answer, I went in. "Mum?" I said anxiously. "Is everything OK?"

Mum had obviously been crying on Jilly's shoulder. She looked up with angry pink-rimmed eyes. "Will you please go away, Fliss," she snivelled. "I really can't cope with any extra hassle today."

I was so hurt, I gave this little gasp.

Then I shut the door and went straight to my bedroom. And even though it was still light, I put on my night things, drew my bedroom curtains and climbed into bed, because you know what?

I couldn't cope with any extra hassle either.

CHAPTER SIX

The first thing I saw when I opened my eyes next morning was a beautiful golden-haired girl, fast asleep in my spare bed.

Yuk! I thought. I've been sharing my oxygen with Awful Amber!

It's amazing what a difference twenty-four hours can make. Yesterday I'd been so sure Amber would turn out to be my dream best friend. I'd even wished it was the holidays, so we could spend more time together. Now it was like I couldn't get away from her fast enough.

I scowled down at her, like a grouchy bear

who just found Goldilocks. Can you believe Amber looks perfect in her sleep? She doesn't even dribble!

I got washed and dressed and went downstairs. I was SO dreading facing Mum. I could only think of one thing which would make someone sob her heart out, five days before her wedding day.

Either Mum or Andy must have decided that getting married was a big mistake. But for some strange reason, they hadn't got around to informing me.

Suddenly I pictured those pretty peachy dresses hanging up in Mum's bedroom. Promise you won't laugh, but in my mind's eye they were *drooping*. I got this huge lump in my throat. My parents' marriage was over before it had even begun.

But when I went into the kitchen, I felt totally confused.

Mum and Andy were in there having a SERIOUS cuddle!! As soon as they saw me, they sprang apart, and I saw Mum had been crying again.

She quickly wiped her eyes. "Fliss, love,"

she said. "Whatever happened last night? Andy came up to ask if you wanted to go with him to get a takeaway, and you were fast asleep."

"Oh, yeah," I said in a casual kind of voice. "I had this headache."

But I was having major pangs of jealousy. Our family only has takeaways like, once a year. But we always get them from the same place – a restaurant called Bamboo, and it's THE best Chinese food, this side of heaven.

Andy sighed. "I'd better go to work." He gave Mum a soul-searching look. "Are you sure you don't want me to stay home, Nikky?"

"No, I'll be fine, love," she said. And another long look passed between them, like they were talking in a code only they understood.

My heart gave a little flutter. They've kissed and made up, I told myself. They had a tiff, that's all. Now everything's cool and groovy again.

And for like five seconds, the five peachy little dresses perked up.

But deep down, my days as an ostrich were strictly numbered. Because if everything was so hunky-dory, why did both my parents still look worried to death?

As Andy went out, Callum came in, yawning. "I stayed up REALLY late," he boasted. "*And* I had Chinese food. YOU didn't, ha ha!" Boys just love to put the boot in, don't they?

"Great," I said drearily.

Callum rubbed his tummy. "Amber let me have her last spring roll," he added. And he swaggered off with his cereal to watch breakfast TV.

Mum grinned. "Callum thinks Amber's great. He actually fell asleep against her shoulder last night."

"Oh, really," I said, in what I hoped was a non-committal voice.

But inside Grouchy Bear was yelling, "Keep your hands off my brother, Goldilocks! He's mine!"

Mum poured me some juice. She kept darting anxious looks at me. "Don't worry. I'll keep Amber entertained while you're at school," she said brightly. "I thought I'd take her and Jilly to Bradgate Park."

"Mmnn," I mumbled.

Mum darted another look from under her lashes. "Erm, Fliss," she said. "About yesterday, when you came in?"

I didn't know what to say, so I had a tiny sip of juice.

Mum laughed. "I think everything just suddenly got on top of me." She was smiling, but her voice had a definite wobble in it.

"Mum, is everything OK?" I blurted out. "I mean you still love Andy, right?"

Mum gasped. "What EVER made you say that, you funny girl?" she asked.

I replayed that moment over and over, all the way to school. What EVER made you say that? What EVER made you say that? Each time, I got the same result.

Captured on my mental video tape, Mum looked and sounded genuinely shocked at my question.

As I saw it, there were three possibilities. Either:

75

1) I REALLY had nothing to worry about.
2) My mum should definitely be put up for Actress of the Year.

Or:

3) My mum was shocked because I'd finally twigged something was wrong.

In other words, the whole situation was still about as clear as mud.

I decided not to tell my friends about my latest worry. It seemed like I was always crying on their shoulders these days. Plus, the Mum and Andy worry was kind of private.

"Hi!" I said brightly, as we all met up at the school gate. "Mum says are you all still on for after school?"

They looked at me as if I was speaking Martian.

"We're going to Leicester, remember? Shopping, then a serious pig-out at Pizza Hut!"

For some reason my friends seemed uncomfortable.

"I'd love to," said Lyndz. "But I've got this stupid thing I have to do."

"Me too," said Frankie. "Not the same thing," she added hastily. "A different stupid thing, that I totally forgot about."

Rose had gone red. "I can't come, either."

Honestly, I felt embarrassed for them. I glared at Kenny. "What about you? Have you got a stupid thing you just remembered you forgot?"

Kenny shook her head. "Uh-uh. The fact is, I don't think I'd enjoy Amber's kind of shopping. Plus, I *totally* wouldn't enjoy her company!"

I stared at them. "But you said you'd love to come!"

"We hadn't met Miss Fabulous then," Kenny pointed out.

"But then it'll just be me and Amber," I said. The thought made me break into a cold sweat.

My friends looked sheepish.

"It's just a shopping trip," I pleaded. "You don't have to marry her. You don't even have to talk to her if you don't want."

"No," said Lyndz unhappily. "But we'd have to listen to her."

77

Frankie put her arm around me. "It's not personal."

"Yeah, right," I said gloomily.

"Just tell your mum you won't go," said Kenny. "That's what I'd do."

I shook my head. "I can't."

"Why not?" everyone said at once.

"Then she'd guess me and Amber don't hit it off."

"So what?" said Kenny. "There's no LAW which says you've got to be buddies with your mum's friend's daughter!"

"It would hurt Mum's feelings," I said.

Kenny rolled her eyes. "Fliss, you are such a lightweight."

I clamped my lips together and counted to ten. You don't know you're born, Laura McKenzie, I thought darkly. You have NO idea what I'm going through.

I think Rosie did, though. She said softly, "Probably Fliss thinks her mum has got enough stress with the wedding and everything."

"Yeah," I said. "I do actually."

"So how's it going with those four

somethings?" Lyndz asked, to change the subject. Then the whistle went and it was time to go into school.

As the day went on, I got more and more depressed. Then on the way home, I had another one of my psychic flashes. This trip was bad news, I just KNEW it.

The instant I stepped inside the house, I heard Amber in full flow. "Nikky, I had the *best* time today. That olde worlde house had such an *awesome* atmosphere! Gosh, I just came out in goosebumps all over!"

I was in the living room by this time, but no-one noticed me for ages. Mum and Jilly were too busy listening to Amber gushing on about Lady Jane's awesome house, until I thought I'd totally throw up!!

I went to give Mum a hug. "Mum," I hissed in her ear. "I'm really tired. Mrs Weaver made us work incredibly hard today. Maybe you should go to Leicester without me."

Mum laughed. "You'll feel better once you get out of those school clothes! I'll give you ten minutes to get changed, then we'll go."

She beamed at Amber. "Once that girl hits the shops, she just shops till she drops."

Amber went into fits of laughter. "Gosh that is SO spooky! Are you sure Felicity and I aren't long-lost twins?"

I looked up in surprise. But it was my mum that Amber was merrily bonding with, not me.

Poor old Callum was looking glum. Patsy had offered to babysit, and I think he was terrified she'd be cooking his tea!

"I'll bring you back a treat," I told him.

"Fizz Bombs," he said at once. "'They blast your buds'. Two packets. No, THREE!"

"Get out fast, before he demands a plane to Cuba," Jilly giggled.

But my brother flung his arms round me, giving me one of his desperate cling-on hugs. Mum had to peel him off me like Velcro. We closed the door on frantic yells of "It's not fair! It's not fair!"

"I'm sorry I didn't meet your friends, Fliss," said Jilly, as we drove out of the village. "Amber's been telling me all about them."

I bet she has, I thought.

Amber was staring out of the window, so I took the opportunity to pull a horrible face. It sounds babyish, but it made me feel a very tiny bit better!

Mum and Jill were nattering about all these people they used to know, back in the days before I was born. People with nicknames like Buzz and Miggsy, so you couldn't tell if they were male or female.

"You're very quiet in the back, girls," Mum said suddenly.

"Uhuh," we both mumbled.

"Not feeling sick are you, Fliss? My daughter suffers from dreadful travel sickness," Mum announced to the world.

Amber rolled her eyes. "Great," she muttered.

"I'm fine," I said stonily. "Don't you worry your head about me."

There was another long silence.

"I don't know what you girls want to do," Mum said at last. "But I've got to find *the* perfect going-away dress, for after the wedding."

"I'll help," said Amber at once. "I know just the style which will suit you. You are so lucky, Nikky. You've got bone structure most supermodels would *die* for."

I watched Mum turning pink in her driving mirror.

"Honestly, all this fuss!" I burst out. "I suppose next you'll have to get a coming-*back* dress? I mean, get real, Mum, you can't close your wardrobe as it is. What do you need *another* dress for?"

You're shocked, aren't you? So was I! I had no IDEA all this spiteful stuff was going to come splurting out of my mouth.

Suddenly Mum went all efficient. "It's probably best if I park in the shopping centre," she said. She gave a hurt little laugh. "If I don't miss the signs, that is."

"Perhaps you'd like me to look out for signs for you, Nikky?" Amber said at once, in her fake helpful voice. "I do that for Mom all the time, back home."

"Would you, Amber? That would be really useful," said Mum warmly.

Goldilocks was the perfect name for that

girl. In the space of one school day, this golden-haired girl wonder had totally taken my place.

Can you see what Amber was doing? She was being ME, only better! The Hollywood version of Felicity Sidebotham – the sweet, helpful, style-conscious daughter of my mother's dreams.

I trailed after them out of the car park, watching them all being giggly girls together. So what was I meant to do now? Disappear in a puff of smoke?

Suddenly this cold rage came over me. Huh, you *wish*, Goldilocks, I growled. So they wanted me to be Amber's long-lost twin, did they? Then that's what I'd be. The scary wicked twin who gets her revenge!!

I really went for it. I sulked and sighed and rolled my eyes all around the shopping centre. I'm not exaggerating. I was so bad, I made Wednesday Addams look like the Milky Bar Kid! Well, OK, so I'm exaggerating slightly. But you get the picture.

The spooky thing was, once I started I totally couldn't stop.

When Mum came out of a cubicle looking drop-dead gorgeous in this sweet dress and asked me what I thought, did I tell her how great she looked? I did not. I just yawned, and said "Whatever," as if I couldn't care less. I hated myself for doing it, but it was like my wicked twin sister had totally taken me over.

And that meant that Amber got to say MY lines. "Andy is going to go crazy when he sees you in that colour," she cooed.

"He'll go even crazier when he sees the bill," I muttered.

Instead of going for pizza, we went to some new pancake parlour Amber liked the sound of. By this time I'd figured out the perfect way to punish Mum for preferring Amber to me. I probably told you, Mum is really diet-conscious? So I ordered this TOTAL calorie-fest. Pancakes, waffles, doughnuts with hot fudge sauce.

Guess what that scheming little Goldilocks did then?

"My, those waffles look so-o good," she cried, like some kid in *The Waltons*. And she ordered EXACTLY the same things!

Our mothers didn't have a clue what was going on. Only Amber and I knew she had just declared war.

The trouble is, I don't like sweet stodgy food that much. And after stuffing my face for fifteen minutes or so, I was already slowing down. But Jilly's daughter kept right on going – dipping, chewing and swallowing.

I've got to admit, all Amber's acting classes had totally paid off. She had this unbelievably innocent expression, like she truly had no idea that she was subjecting me to Death by Doughnut!

Not only that, but my revenge ploy didn't even *work*. Mum actually thought it was funny. She and Jilly got all misty-eyed about the night they stayed at a friend's house, and Jilly got this sudden chocolate craze, and Miggsy (or maybe Buzz) baked them this amazingly gooey cake.

"The trouble was, it wasn't ready until after midnight," Mum giggled. "We were dying to go to bed, but she refused to let us go to sleep until we'd eaten every last crumb!"

Mum always gives everyone the impression she was a real Nikky No-Mates when she was growing up. Now it seemed she'd been sharing midnight cake with crowds of kids, all with cool and groovy nicknames. It made me feel like I didn't really know her.

Quite suddenly I pushed my plate away.

"I think Fliss has had enough," said Amber sweetly. "Don't worry, it won't go to waste."

And she actually took my last doughnut off my plate and popped it into her mouth!!

If I wasn't feeling so miserable (also REALLY sick), I'd have shoved her smiling face right into my plate, saying, "Then DO have the rest of my sauce, Amber, while you're at it!"

But we both knew she'd won, so I just stared straight ahead, waiting for my ordeal to end.

Only it didn't.

That night Mum came to find me in the kitchen, where I was gulping down water, trying to dilute the ill-effects of my fudge-fest.

"Sweetheart," she said. "I've got something to tell you."

I had my second psychic flash of the day. You're not going to like this, Fliss, I thought.

"The thing is, Jilly isn't just my best friend. She's a real soul mate," Mum blurted out.

I stared at her.

"And that makes Amber really special too," she said awkwardly. "Which is why I want her to be one of my bridesmaids."

"You're kidding," I whispered.

"I realise this is a bit sudden," said Mum. "But I just know it would make Jilly really happy."

I didn't plan to sit down – it was more like my legs gave way underneath me, so that I kind of fell into a kitchen chair. My head was spinning with all this urgent stuff I needed to say. But in the end, I just croaked, "But there's only five dresses."

"I know," said Mum sadly. "It's a shame, but there it is."

I couldn't speak. It had been touch and go for some time, but the happy sparkling wedding of my dreams had finally morphed into a total nightmare.

Because in order for Awful Amber to be a bridesmaid, one of my friends would have to stand down.

CHAPTER SEVEN

You know those agony aunts they have in women's magazines? We just *lurve* reading out those letters, don't you? Kenny swears they're made up. She says no-one in their right MINDS would parade their bizarre personal problems for complete strangers to snigger over.

There's two reasons Kenny believes this.

1) She never watches those totally riveting American chat shows.

And:

2) Unlike me, she is not a girl who easily gets her knickers in a twist.

It's like that shopping trip mix-up. My other friends fibbed themselves blue in the face, trying not to hurt my feelings. But Kenny just came clean, like it was no biggie. I'd LOVE to be more like Kenny. I really would. (I just wouldn't want to DRESS like her! *Miaow!*)

But that night when I'd closed my diary (my deadly secret one) and finally switched off my torch, I lay in the dark, composing a letter to some wise agony aunt in the sky.

Dear Auntie Whoever,

Due to circumstances beyond my control, I must inform my friends that one of them can no longer be a bridesmaid at my mother's wedding. I have absolutely no idea how to do this without hurting someone's feelings, and maybe even losing a friend. Can you help? Also, could you please reply by tomorrow, which is when I have to break this disappointing news?

Yours sincerely

Felicity Sidebotham

But by the time I'd finished, I realised that it wasn't an agony aunt I needed after all. What I needed was a miracle.

I could hear gentle breathing from the other side of the room, final proof that Amber totally didn't have a heart. After what she'd done to me, it just didn't seem fair that she was sleeping like a baby. *I* was the innocent person here. So how come it was *me* tossing and turning all night long?

I don't know about you, but when I have a bad night, with the flu or something, I'm usually longing for the first signs of morning. But that night, I was dreading the moment when the sky changed colour over Cuddington and all the little birds began to tweet.

Because I knew that no matter how miserable I felt tonight, it was nothing LIKE as bad as I was going to feel tomorrow.

Don't worry, I promise to spare you the rest of the depressing details.

I'm going to fast forward to the part where I was getting dressed for school – in the bathroom, actually, because not only was

Amber using up my oxygen without permission, she'd also totally invaded my privacy.

And as I finished brushing my hair and putting it up in a tidy school ponytail (Mum says a girl should never let herself go, no matter HOW bad she feels), I looked my reflection in the eye.

"Fliss," I said bravely. "Here's your chance to become a stronger, better person, just like Kenny. These are your friends. Just tell them the truth, OK? They'll understand."

My bathroom resolution lasted all the way to school. Right up till the moment I joined my friends in the playground.

The minute she saw me coming, Frankie started humming. The others all joined in, grinning. You won't need me to tell you that this was not the ideal moment for my mates to break into *Here Comes the Bride*.

They looked so incredibly happy that I almost burst into tears. How could Mum make me hurt my friends like this?

"Oh, hi," I said, trying to force a smile.

Rosie giggled. "We've all been getting

totally over-excited, Flissy! We just realised there's only THREE days to go before You Know What!"

"I SO hope I don't get hiccups at the vital moment!" Lyndz bubbled.

Kenny rolled her eyes. "Don't we all," she agreed.

But I'd stopped listening. Suddenly, in a flash of inspiration, I knew where my miracle was coming from. It wasn't like she WANTED to be a bridesmaid, I told myself. I'd practically had to beg her. She'd only agreed in the first place because I went on and on about how much it mattered to me.

As I turned to Kenny, I could already feel a big smile spreading over my face. Miracles happened. They did. You heard about them all the time.

"What about you, Kenz?" I said casually. "Don't tell me you're dying to climb into that meringue, because I won't believe you."

Kenny grinned. "Then you're wrong, Miss Smarty Pants. I know I wasn't keen to begin with. But now I wouldn't miss it for the world."

"Oh," I said. "That's so, erm – sweet." I heard myself sounding like a total fake.

Can you believe it took me until lunchtime to pluck up the courage to tell them the truth? By then I'd worked myself into such a state, I was in extreme danger of going into orbit.

I waited until everyone had finished eating. Everyone except me, that is. I was so nervous, I couldn't eat a thing.

"I think someone's got wedding jitters," grinned Frankie.

I'll do it fast, I thought. Then maybe it won't hurt so much. So in the end, I took a big breath, and blurted out the whole sorry story.

It's weird. I was prepared for just about every reaction, except the one I got. They didn't believe me. Everyone fell about laughing.

"Nice one, Fliss," Kenny chortled. "You really had us going there."

Rosie clutched her chest. "You bad girl!" she giggled. "You gave me a total heart attack!"

"Flissy, sometimes you have the weirdest sense of humour!" said Lyndz in a wondering tone.

Then Frankie's face changed. "She isn't joking," she said. "Look at her!"

Everyone stared at me, and I saw all the laughter go out of their eyes. Tears prickled behind my lids.

"Your mum actually told you to like, SACK one of us to make room for Awful Amber?" gasped Lyndz.

I nodded, and two hot little tears trickled down my cheeks. I kept seeing their happy faces as they sang *Here Comes the Bride*. Now all my friends looked like I'd slapped them.

"Did your mum say which bridesmaid is getting the sack?" Rosie asked finally.

"No," I choked. "She said we've got to figure it out amongst ourselves."

"But HOW?" said Lyndz.

"I don't know," I wept. "I can't believe this is even happening."

I was longing for my friends to comfort me. But they just went scarily quiet. And for a few seconds no-one looked at anyone else.

Then, still carefully not looking at anyone, Rosie said, "Well, I suppose it's got to be Kenny. I mean, we all remember what a terrible time Fliss had getting her to put on a bridesmaid's dress in the first place, right?"

Kenny looked hurt. "How come you're talking about me as if I'm not here?" she demanded in a huffy voice. "But then I suppose you wish I wasn't."

"Don't be stupid, Kenz," said Frankie at once.

Rosie scowled. "I was only saying that it's not fair for one of US to miss out, when everyone knows Kenny hates dressing up and being girly."

Kenny stared at her. "One of US?" she blazed. "What does that mean, exactly? I mean, one of US can't play Let's Dress Up, so suddenly I'm like this ALIEN creature who isn't US?"

"I don't think that's – that's what Rosie meant," I stuttered miserably.

Kenny scraped back her chair.

"I wondered what that was all about this morning," she said in a shaky voice. "All that rhubarb about me and my meringue. It was because you didn't have the guts to tell me the truth!"

"Sssh, Kenny," said Rosie uncomfortably. "Everyone's looking."

But Kenny didn't stop for breath. "Why didn't you just say, 'Laura McKenzie, you'll make a rubbish bridesmaid, so you're FIRED!'" she screamed. Then she ran out of the hall, sobbing as if her heart would break.

The M&Ms must have thought Christmas had come early. It was obvious they were lapping up every moment of our misery.

Then I saw Frankie and Lyndz both glaring at me.

"This is your fault, Felicity Sidebotham," Frankie choked. "I'll never *forgive* you for hurting Kenny's feelings like that."

"Me neither," said Lyndz.

"Hey!" said Rosie. "It's not Flissy's fault if her mum got a bee in her bonnet about Amber being a bridesmaid."

But Frankie and Lyndz just pushed back their chairs and stalked out of the hall.

Have you ever been so upset that you

can't even cry? I sat there at that table with my elbows in everyone's crumbs, the whole school staring at me, and I really wished I could die.

Yet it was like I couldn't even find the energy to get up and leave.

It had all happened so FAST! Like Andy's precious mirror, the Sleepover Club had just shattered into pieces, and I didn't understand *why*. I didn't even know whose fault it was. Was it Amber's, or Mum's, or was it really all down to me, like Frankie said?

As we left the hall, Rosie tucked her arm through mine. "I'm your friend, Fliss," she said fiercely. "I don't care what they say."

All the rest of the day, Kenny sat by herself at the back of the class. I wanted to go up to her and explain that she'd totally got it wrong. But she looked so blank and cold, I didn't dare. It was like she'd put up an invisible force-field which totally stopped the rest of us going near her.

Lyndz and Frankie sat together. When Mrs Weaver wasn't looking, they whispered to each other, darting poisonous looks at me and Rosie.

Without any warning, tears started splashing down my face. Some of them fell on my rough book, smudging the sum I'd been working out in pencil. I scrubbed my hand across my face.

"Don't cry," Rosie whispered. "It'll be OK. I know it will."

I truly couldn't see how. I still believed in miracles and everything. I just didn't think one could happen to me.

That evening I shut myself in the kitchen. I'd told Mum I'd got this work I absolutely had to finish, and that Mrs Weaver would skin me alive if I didn't hand it in by tomorrow. But it was actually because I couldn't stand the thought of spending another evening with Amber and Patsy.

Anyway, there I was, miserably doodling felt-tip hearts on the inside of my work book, when suddenly the phone rang.

It was for Mum. I wasn't in the mood for eavesdropping, to be honest, but I got the vague impression someone had given her some upsetting news. A few minutes after she'd replaced the receiver, the phone rang again. And after Mum had heard what this caller had to say, she sounded totally distraught.

She burst into the kitchen, looking as white as a sheet.

"Did you know about this?" she demanded. "I've just had Frankie and Lyndz's mothers on the phone. Apparently their daughters can no longer perform their bridesmaids' duties on Saturday."

I know it sounds heartless, but I almost burst out laughing. I couldn't help it. Sometimes my friends take my breath away. That's the Sleepover Club all over, I thought. One out, ALL out!

Luckily Mum was too busy ranting to notice my reaction. "What's going on, Fliss?" she blazed. "Have you had some kind of stupid quarrel or something?"

I jumped to my feet. "Stupid *quarrel*!" I screamed. "It's not *us* who's stupid. *You're* the one who forced me to choose between my friends, remember?"

"I didn't do anything of the kind—" Mum began.

"Yes, you did!" I yelled. "You FORCED me. And you know what? I'm proud of my friends for taking a stand. That's what I should have done in the first place. But it's OK, because I'm doing it now!"

I glared at her, breathing hard.

Mum looked alarmed. "What do you mean?" she gasped.

All at once I knew exactly what I was going to say. "It's up to you," I said. "You can have ALL of the Sleepover Club for your bridesmaids, or none of them."

I wasn't shouting now. I was as quiet and reasonable as can be.

"You've got to make up your mind, Mum," I told her calmly. "Is it Amber you want at your wedding? Or is it me?"

CHAPTER EIGHT

It was true what I said to Mum. I should have stood up for my mates at the start. But now that I'd finally done it, I felt like a new person. All my mixed-up feelings melted away like a bad dream, and I knew exactly what I had to do next. But I didn't have much time to do it.

I quickly abandoned my pretend homework, and went to hunt out this fancy writing set which my Auntie Paula gave me last Christmas.

It was the first time I'd used it, actually.

I don't mean to sound ungrateful, but I wasn't too thrilled when I first got it, so I didn't look at it that closely. But as I stripped off the cellophane, I suddenly noticed an eerie coincidence.

My notepaper and envelopes were decorated with cute little cartoons of baby angels. There was also a motto which said, "*Angels fly because they take themselves lightly.*" Isn't that SWEET! Don't tell anyone, but I truly felt like those angels had just popped up to show me I was on the right track.

I was incredibly sleepy after my bad night, but I forced my eyes to stay open until I'd written four letters, one for each of my friends, explaining what I'd just told my mum.

Then I slipped the sealed envelopes into my school bag and zipped it shut. I didn't think it was wise to leave them lying around. If Amber thought it was OK to muscle in on my mates' bridesmaids' dresses, she *might* figure it was OK to read people's letters too.

I went to bed, convinced I'd found the perfect way to put things right. But so far, it was just a theory.

*   *   *

When I actually went into our classroom next day, I almost lost my nerve. It was like walking into this like, icy wall of HATE. When Lyndz and Frankie saw me coming, they immediately pulled faces, as if I was this really bad smell. But I think you'd have been really proud of me, because I didn't go to pieces. I just reminded myself that the angels were rooting for us all to get back together, then I quickly handed my mates their pink envelopes.

Frankie looked as if I'd dropped a dead mouse in her lap. "What's *this*?" she said in disgust. But she told me afterwards that she was wild with curiosity to know what I was up to, because I'd had such a weird expression on my face!

The four girls read their letters under their desks, while I tried not to look. And I got this sinking feeling. What if it didn't work?

My friends must all read at the same speed or something, because suddenly I heard these soft little sighs as they all reached the last line together.

Then to Mrs Weaver's astonishment, Lyndz, Frankie and Kenny jumped out of their seats and rushed over to gave me a hug. (Rosie was sitting next to me already, if you remember!)

We had to wait till break before we could have our proper reunion, but it was well worth waiting for. Everyone was SO emotional, it wasn't true!! For ten solid minutes, we all cried and hugged and mushily forgave each other. You should have seen us!

"I can't believe you stood up to her like that!" sniffled Frankie. "That was SO brave, Flissy."

I blew my nose hard. "It didn't feel brave," I said. Which was true. "I just couldn't bear the thought of everyone breaking friends, because of me."

And we all had another round of hugs.

But Kenny looked thoughtful. "Fliss, it's so brilliant, what you did. But I really don't think you should back out of your own mum's wedding."

"Nor do I," said Lyndz.

Rosie shook her head. "Me neither."

"I've got an idea," said Frankie suddenly. "We'll put our names in a hat, and whoever Fliss picks out has to stand down."

"Cool," Kenny grinned. "Except we haven't actually *got* a hat."

"Couldn't we use something else?" asked Lyndz.

"I suppose," said Frankie doubtfully. "It just seems more official with an actual hat, somehow."

"We could borrow one from the dressing-up box?" suggested Lyndz.

We all went dashing off to ask Mrs Dwyer – she's one of the infant teachers.

She looked dead suspicious at first. I could see her thinking, "What ARE these weird girls up to now?"

But then Frankie went on about how it was like, the ONLY possible way for us to reach the most important democratic decision in the history of the Sleepover Club, and Mrs Dwyer eventually gave in.

We had four hats to choose from. A straw hat with little daisies and violets on, a beefeater's furry busby, a Red Baron-type pilot's cap with fleecy ear-flaps, and an ancient Roman helmet.

We went for the helmet in the end. As Frankie said, despite being plastic, it was by far the most dignified.

Mrs Dwyer tactfully left us alone in the Year One classroom, while everyone wrote their names on pieces of scrap paper, folded them into squares, and popped them into the Roman helmet.

I shut my eyes, felt around, and drew out one of the squares.

"It's Frankie," I said. "Sorry, Frankie," I added, guiltily.

"Yeah, sorry Frankie," mumbled everyone, though you could see they were all really thrilled that I hadn't picked them!

But to my surprise Frankie took the news really well. "Hey, cheer up," she grinned bravely. "I mean, I'm still coming to the wedding, right?"

Honestly, Frankie's like a different person since her little sister, Izzy, was born. I'm not being mean, but the old Frankie was a typical only child, always expecting to have everything her way. These days she's so mellow, it's unbelievable.

"Does everyone want to come back to my place after school, to tell Mum the good news?" I asked.

I hadn't really spoken to Mum since last night, I realised.

"I bet she was seriously stressed when you told her," said Rosie.

"I'll say," I said. "But everything's been stressing her out lately, I don't know why."

"Weddings are most peculiar things," said Lyndz, putting on a doddery old lady's voice.

"TELL me about it," I grinned.

Miss Dwyer put her head round the door. "Reached that world-shattering democratic decision yet, girls?"

"Yes, thanks!" we yelled.

"Well, praise the Lord and give me my classroom back!" she sighed. She stood aside and a horde of over-excited infants came thundering into the class, all yelling "YAY!" at the tops of their voices.

"Infants are so much smaller than you

think, aren't they?" said Lyndz, as we went back into the playground.

"And they have so much fun," sighed Rosie.

Then we had one of our amazing telepathic moments. We all grinned at each other, and we did something really babyish.

All five of us linked arms and ran across the playground, yelling "YAY!" too!

Further down the playground, the M&Ms were talking to Alana Palmer. As we drew level, all three girls narrowed their eyes at us. It's one of their favourite expressions, and it makes them look exactly like those spiteful Siamese cats in *The Lady and the Tramp*.

"See ya!" Lyndz yelled merrily, as we zoomed past.

"But we wouldn't wanna BE ya!" I added.

And we all cracked up laughing.

I was so happy to be back with my friends, I can't tell you. In a funny way, it seemed as if our quarrel had brought us closer together than ever.

We walked home after school, chatting

and teasing each other, just like always. Plus, we kept telling Frankie what a star she was for the way she'd taken not being a bridesmaid. By the time we reached my house, she was practically walking on air!

But that's NOTHING to how Mum looked when we told her the good news! She was totally *ecstatic*. She insisted on hugging everyone, but I don't think they minded too much.

"I promise you'll still get your special bridesmaid present, Frankie," Mum said.

"Oh, goody," said Frankie greedily, and we all burst out laughing.

After everyone had gone, I gave Mum a specially huge hug to make up for our fight. "Everything's going to be all right from now on," I told her.

A flicker of worry crossed her face. "I hope you're right," she whispered.

"I KNOW I'm right," I said. "Actually, I think I'm getting psychic powers."

Mum gave a tired grin. "Good," she said. "I could really use them."

My mother meant it to come out as a joke,

but I could hear the same scared little wobble in her voice that I'd noticed before.

I watched her anxiously as she rinsed and chopped vegetables for a salad, hoping for clues to her odd behaviour.

Whatever could it be that was making her act so sad and faraway? And why oh *why* wouldn't she tell me? Mum and I always used to share everything. What could be so terrible, I wondered, that she had to keep it such a dark and deadly secret?

After tea, Mum made Amber try on Frankie's bridesmaid's dress.

She revolved slowly, like a cake on a cake-stand, as Mum fiddled around, twitching at seams and yanking down the hem.

Amber's the kind of girl who couldn't look bad if she was covered in slime. Even so, I couldn't help feeling just a tiny bit smug. That dress didn't look anything LIKE as good on Amber as it had done on Frankie!

I don't know why, but all at once, Amber didn't seem nearly such a pain. She didn't mention her fabulous boyfriend once, all night. She also helped me wash up. Though

I'm not sure if these things actually triggered my new tolerant attitude, or whether hating Amber was just getting too much like hard work.

Plus, it had dawned on me that after the wedding, Jilly's daughter would be out of my life forever, but my great friends and my family would all still be here. Anyway, that night, for the first time, Amber and I actually AGREED on something.

We both desperately wanted to watch this funny film on TV, but no-one else was keen, so we watched it on the set in my room. To start with, we were both a bit on our dignity. It was like neither of us wanted to be the first person to laugh out loud. We'd snigger, then instantly straighten our faces. But the film was so silly that soon we were both howling with laughter.

When it was over, Amber went off to use the bathroom, and I trotted downstairs to say goodnight to Mum and Andy.

To my dismay, Andy's mum followed me out into the hall. "I want a private word, Felicity," she whispered.

Oh-oh, I thought. I should have guessed it was all too good to be true. What have I done wrong *now*?

Whatever it was, Patsy didn't want anyone else to hear about my crimes, because she put her finger to her lips and kind of shunted me mysteriously into the kitchen. Then she shut the door.

Did I say before that Patsy always looks and sounds slightly offended?

"I just wanted to tell you," she said in her stiff way, "that I'm really proud of you, dear."

I was so expecting an earbashing that I actually glanced behind me, to see who Patsy was really talking to! "Proud?" I said bewildered. "Of me?"

"You've got strong principles," she said. "I like that. And you're a true friend."

"Oh," I croaked. "Thanks, erm, Patsy."

"I'd like you to bring Francesca back here after school tomorrow. If everything goes according to plan, I may have a surprise for her." And Patsy had this real glint in her eye, like she was actually enjoying our little conspiracy. It was the exact same look Andy

113

gets sometimes, when he's winding Mum up!

"OK," I said, surprised. "I'll ask her."

I couldn't think *what* Patsy was being so cloak-and-dagger about. But I really REALLY hoped her plan wouldn't involve cabbage soup.

I was so tired by the time I switched out my light that I almost fell asleep as soon as I hit the pillow.

Only almost.

Because just as I drifted happily away to dreamland, it hit me!

I'd only got two days until the wedding! And not only had I failed to come up with any of my four somethings, but I still had no IDEA what I was going to get Mum and Andy for a present.

I thumped my pillow angrily.

Felicity Sidebotham, you total fluff-brain! I fumed to myself. How COULD you have forgotten something so important!!

CHAPTER NINE

Bet you thought I was telling serious porkies, didn't you, when I said this story was going to be like a rollercoaster ride! Bet you've changed your mind now though, eh? And guess what! The thrills and spills aren't nearly over yet.

But as this story is being told by that well-known butterfly-brain Felicity Sidebotham, I thought you might be feeling a bit confused by this time. So I thought I'd remind you EXACTLY where we've got up to now, in the wedding countdown. Can you believe it's now actually the day before the wedding?

Me neither!

Have you ever been so incredibly excited, that nothing actually feels quite real? Isn't it the weirdest sensation in the world?

That Friday, I got up and kind of floated through the motions of my usual routine, but it was like I was watching myself in a movie, do you know what I mean? Fliss gets ready for school. Fliss leaves the house. Fliss walks down the street with a soppy grin on her face, dreaming of peach satin dresses, wedding cake and confetti!

"My mother is getting married tomorrow," I whispered, as I walked down the same village street I walked down every day. But I'd been waiting so long, it was like I couldn't really believe my dream was finally turning into reality.

Then I remembered that I still had my little mystery to solve. At break, I took Frankie aside and gave her Patsy's message.

She looked amazed. "Why me?"

"I have no idea," I said truthfully.

"Didn't she even give you like, a tiny CLUE what it's about?"

"She said she might have a surprise for you. So can you come?" I asked anxiously.

Frankie grinned. "Do I *look* like a girl who'd pass up the opportunity for a mystery surprise?"

The great thing about this particular Friday was that as well as being Mum's wedding day minus one, it also happened to be the last day of term. This meant we had no actual lessons, YIPPEE! Which, as Kenny said, was really just as well, seeing as by this time all five of us were in like, dizzy nonstop orbit around Planet Wedding!

Frankie and I walked home together, trying to guess what on earth Patsy's surprise could be. Some of our guesses got pretty wild!

"It's her secret recipe for cabbage soup," Frankie suggested. "It's so hush-hush, she's going to write it down in code and make me learn it off by heart. After that she'll make me swallow it. And if I don't, I needn't think I'm going to get ANY pudding!"

"No, I know what it is," I giggled. "You've won an entire five minutes at the Patsy

Proudlove Charm School!"

But the joke was on us, as it turned out.

Andy's mum called out to us as we were coming in through the front door. "We're in the living room, dears," she said. And if it had been anyone else but Andy's mum, I'd have sworn she sounded excited.

Frankie followed me in. "Hi, everyone," she beamed. Then her face kind of crumpled. "Oh, hi Amber," she said bravely. "Wow, that dress really suits you."

No WONDER poor old Frankie didn't know where to look.

Amber was striking this really haughty pose beside the window. But that's not all. She was only wearing her bridesmaid's dress, would you believe! Talk about rubbing Frankie's nose in it. Amber couldn't have been more tactless if she'd tried. Though in passing, I DID notice that the dress looked heaps better on her than it had last night. I hated to admit it, but she looked completely amazing.

OK, now I'm going to let you in on the big secret, right?

In case you hadn't guessed, Mum, Patsy, Jilly and Amber had cooked up a wicked little plot between them. Unknown to Frankie and me, Amber was totally acting her socks off. To be honest, she was the only plotter who managed to keep a straight face (I put it down to all those acting lessons!).

Mum, Jilly and Patsy did TRY to look innocent, bless them. But their twinkly eyes just wouldn't co-operate. So it soon became obvious, even to us, that something very fishy was going on.

Suddenly Frankie couldn't stand the suspense another second. "So is anyone going to tell me about this surprise or what?" she blurted.

"Da-DA," sang Mum, and she whipped a second bridesmaid's dress from behind her back.

Frankie and I stared at it, hopelessly confused.

"Patsy and Amber have been working so hard while you were at school. They really ought to get medals," said Mum.

"It was Patsy's idea," Amber chipped in.

"I still don't get it," I said. "What idea?"

"To make a new dress for Amber, of course," beamed Mum. "Patsy and Amber just didn't think it was right for Frankie to miss out."

And my mum presented the dress to a totally stunned Frankie.

"You mean I can still be your bridesmaid after all?" she gasped.

Mum nodded, beaming.

"Wow!" Frankie breathed. Then she rushed at my mum and hugged her madly around the middle. "Thank you SO much," she said in a muffled voice. "This is a very very happy moment and I think I'm going to cry."

That's one way in which Frankie hasn't changed at all. She's still a TOTAL drama queen!

Amber stepped forward. For the first time since I'd met her she looked really unsure of herself. "Can I hug Frankie too?" she said. "I mean, since we're both going to be bridesmaids now."

All this time, Patsy had been busily inspecting her nails, but suddenly she went zooming towards the door. "I think I'll just go and make everyone a nice pot of tea," she called over her shoulder.

But I got the definite feeling she just wanted to get WAY out of hugging range! And for the first time, it occurred to me that Patsy's prickly hedgehog routine was actually terminal shyness.

"But how did they manage to do it so fast?" I said. "No offence, Mum, but it's taken you AGES to make those other dresses."

"Aha," grinned Jilly. "You obviously haven't heard about Patsy's secret past!"

"Apparently Patsy used to be some kind of dressmaker in London," Amber explained.

Mum acted shocked. "Dressmaker! Patsy used to work for a major French fashion house, darling!"

"So making one itty bitty bridesmaid's dress was not exactly a major problem for her," Jilly explained.

"I don't know what we'd have done without her," sighed Mum. "Patsy's worked absolute miracles today."

I started to giggle. I couldn't help it.

"What?" said everyone.

But it wasn't a thought I could exactly share with them, seeing as Patsy herself had just sailed back in with the tea-things. I DID tell it to my Wedding Diary though, before I went to sleep. Want to see what I wrote?

I kept saying I needed a miracle. It just NEVER occurred to me that a miracle could ever come through someone as scary as Patsy! Maybe that's what our vicar means when he says, "God works in mysterious ways"!!

After Frankie went home, Amber and I figured that the grown-ups in the house were all far too busy with wedding preparations to do anything about food. So we sneaked a tub of Ben and Jerry's Rainforest Crunch out of the freezer, grabbed a spoon each, and went up to my room.

But there wasn't really much on TV and gradually we got talking. Actually it turned into a real heart-to-heart.

"You must have thought I was a real pill," Amber said suddenly.

"Oh, er, not really," I said politely.

She laughed. "Sure you did. The fact is, I was incredibly jealous."

"Yeah, right," I said. "You live in LA, next door to Mickey Mouse and – and lots of other famous people whose names I can't remember just now, and you're jealous of *me*. That makes sense. NOT!"

"Sorry to disappoint you, Fliss, but me and Mickey don't actually hang out on a regular basis," Amber teased. Then she sighed. "I do have a great life though, and I wouldn't change it. Except for one thing."

I stared at her.

"I wish I had great friends, like you guys," she said. "The first time I heard you going on about them, it made me feel kind of lonely." I could tell Amber meant it too. Her voice had this husky little catch in it.

"Don't you have loads of friends in LA?" I said.

Amber grinned. "Don't look so worried. I'm not like, a total hermit or anything. But none of my friends really *know* me. Not the way you guys know each other."

"We have these huge fights sometimes," I said.

"Yeah, but you make up, right?" Amber helped herself to a mega spoonful of Rainforest Crunch. "I did have this really cool friend, once," she said. "Her name was Lauren McGravy."

"You're kidding."

"No, I swear. That's her real name." Amber went into a fit of giggles. "Poor Lauren," she said. "She's allergic to everything, so she's like, sneezing constantly. But this is totally not a human sneeze, right? It sounds like it's made by some cute little Disney cartoon." And she did a wicked imitation of a Lauren McGravy-type sneeze.

"What happened to her?"

She sighed. "The usual thing. Lauren's parents split and her mother took her off to New York."

"You can still phone," I suggested.

"Yeah, yeah," said Amber. "I call her up sometimes. I just hate how after you put down the receiver, you feel like twenty times more lonely than you did before."

There was quite a long silence after she said this. It wasn't a seriously squirm-making silence, but I got the feeling that Amber felt a bit down in the dumps. So it was probably best not to ask her any more about Lauren McGravy just yet.

"Hey," I said suddenly. "There's a really mushy film on later. Want to watch it with me?"

Amber's eyes lit up. "How mushy?" she demanded. "You know, on a scale of one to ten?"

"Twelve at *least*," I giggled.

She wriggled her toes. "I can't WAIT," she said gleefully.

Just then Andy yelled upstairs. Luckily for all our rumbly tummies, my thoughtful step-dad had brought back a carload of pizza for everyone.

"I know it's not very healthy," Mum kept saying merrily, as she handed round massive slices dripping with melted mozzarella cheese. "I'm so disorganised today. But it can't be helped."

She caught me staring at her.

"What?" she said. "I've got tomato sauce on my nose again, haven't I?"

"No," I said. "It's nothing, honestly."

But a wave of wonderful relief washed over me.

Mum was totally her old self again. The scared little wobble in her voice had disappeared. All those stress crinkles in her forehead had been smoothed out. And though she was only wearing the teeniest touch of make-up, my mother looked exactly like brides are supposed to look.

For the first time in over a week, she was really and truly radiant.

And with one of my psychic flashes, I knew I totally didn't need to worry about her scary secret any more. I could tell that it was now well and truly over, and that's all that mattered.

By the way, Amber and I never did get to watch that mushy film.

You see, while we were stuffing ourselves with pizza, I had a private word with Patsy, who immediately set us to work on a secret late-night project. And you're just going to have to wait till the end of the story before I tell you what the project was!

"Mind if I keep the light on?" I asked Amber, when we finally got to bed some time after midnight. "I want to write in my diary for a while."

"I don't know how you can keep your eyes open," she yawned. "I'm exhausted. That Patsy is *such* a slave-driver."

She settled down to sleep, and I started scribbling in my Wedding Diary. I showed you some of this stuff earlier. Plus I also wrote this:

This has been the most amazing week of my life. And now it's almost over, I feel much older and a (tiny) bit wiser. It's like I had this fairy tale going on in my head, where Amber was the beautiful princess who totally didn't have a heart. And I definitely had Patsy pegged as the mean old witch with her evil potions and scary ways!

Well, it turns out I was wrong. (Though Andy's mum does have very useful magic powers. Heh heh heh!)

And here's the icing on the cake. I successfully completed my mission, yippee! Thanks to Patsy's powers, those four somethings are totally sorted. Not only has the wicked ladder spell finally been broken, but I've also got a completely fab and groovy wedding present for Andy and Mum – it's

Oops, I only just shut my diary in time or I'd have ruined the big surprise! I'm not being funny, but I truly can't let you read any more, just yet. These are like, official wedding secrets, OK? Which means they can only be unveiled at the actual wedding!

Are you KIDDING? Of course you're invited. I'm just working up to the most exciting bit of the whole story, you nutcase!

So jump back on the wedding rollercoaster, and get ready to go "ooh!" and "aah!" and "wow!" because that great big water splash is coming up, any minute NOW!

CHAPTER TEN

This is SO embarrassing.

I've been building up to this like, HUGE moment in my story, and now I've come over all wobbly.

It's not just stage fright. You see, in the middle of the celebrations, I got some news which completely blew me away. I took it really calmly at the time. But now I'm in this total DAZE.

I mean, I've been talking all along like this was just about Mum's wedding. But it turns out that the whole time, there was this other mega dramatic stuff going on behind the scenes. So now I'm feeling like, "Fliss, how could you be so DIM!"

OK, OK, I'm probably being about as clear as mud! But my head is just spinning. If you could see my thought bubbles, like in those cartoon strips, I just know they'd be totally haywire.

Bubble 1 is panicking: "Eek, NOW where do I start?"

Bubble 2 is signalling frantically: "Major headache, major headache! A fluff-brain like you shouldn't be attempting to describe the sheer wonderfulness of Mum's Big Day, let alone explaining this like, WILD new strand of the plot!"

But inside Bubble 3 is just a humungous exclamation mark!

In case you were wondering, that's the part of my brain which is still trying to digest my stunning news. You see, it *seemed* to come out of the blue. But, now I look back, I realise there were all these clues staring me in the face, which I totally failed to pick up on.

Phew! Thanks for letting me get that off my

chest. Actually, I think I've calmed down very slightly. So I'll tell you what we're going to do. We'll put my big news on the back burner for now, and just carry on like I originally planned.

So now we're going to zoom straight to that hopelessly mushy scene we've all been waiting for.

The one where we FINALLY get to see (SIGH!!) Mum's dress!

The night before the wedding, Mum had firmly packed Andy off to stay with Dave, Andy's best man. So apart from Callum (who doesn't exactly rate as a real bloke), this was like, an *exclusively* girly moment.

Patsy had been shut in with Mum practically since DAWN, helping her get ready. So there was just Jilly and all six of us bridesmaids, waiting nervously for Mum to come downstairs.

But when she eventually appeared at the top of the stairs, I almost cried. I'm not lying. We all just stared and stared at her, until she came over all shy.

"Do I look all right?" she asked anxiously.

131

But I think she knew the answer really.

"You look like a fairy-tale princess," sighed Frankie.

Mum had chosen a dress which was utterly perfect for a summer wedding. It was in shimmery ivory satin, with slightly puffy sleeves which came to just below her elbows. The skirt was completely plain, but the sleeves and bodice had all these tiny embroidered hearts and roses done in silver thread, plus silver beads so tiny, you'd hardly know they were there at all.

Oh, and you should have seen Mum's veil! It was the dreamiest thing. It was really long, and edged with more teeny roses and scattered with little seed pearls. To keep it in place, she'd got this gorgeous silver tiara with a cluster of larger pearls in the centre.

Her flowers were really simple – just this absolute *cascade* of creamy blossoms. They smelled so lovely, it seemed like the dress itself was giving off some unique wedding-day scent.

And if Frankie and the others think that sounds soppy, well, that's just too bad. My mum was getting married. I'm *supposed* to feel like that!

Oops, I almost forgot to tell you about her amazing train!

Actually, none of us realised exactly *how* amazing until Mum reached the bottom of the stairs, and suddenly there was absolutely NO room in our hall!

In case you didn't know, most people have at *least* one rehearsal before their actual wedding day, so everyone knows what they've got to do. But for very special reasons I'll go into later, Mum and Andy's schedule was so hectic that they totally couldn't fit one in.

Anyway, you've got to picture like, MILES of satin, all billowing around the hall of our little semi!

Well, naturally we all went into a major panic! I mean, Mum's special wedding car was arriving in five minutes. In other words, the Peaches and Cream Squad (Jilly's nickname for Mum's bridesmaids!) had precisely five minutes to acquire some serious train-management skills!

Poor Mum looked like she might pass out cold at this point.

But Patsy quickly calmed everyone down, explaining that it was really just a question of common sense.

"But you *must* stop walking the instant Nikky stands still," she told us sternly. "And don't lag too far behind, or else you'll all get dragged along behind her like a bunch of bad water-skiers."

This was such a wild picture that my mother and all six bridesmaids, me included, burst into mad fits of giggles. Jilly immediately whipped out her Polaroid camera and took a snap of us all, falling about hysterically, in our long dresses and flowery crowns.

There was only just enough time left for Mum to give us all our special bridesmaids' lockets. They were on these incredibly fine gold chains with the SWEETEST tiny gold hearts on.

"Aaah," said Jilly when we'd put them on. "That is the perfect finishing touch, Nikky. Don't they all look cute!"

I was so proud of Kenny. I mean, imagine Laura MaKenzie allowing herself to be seen in public *looking cute*. That is TRUE friendship!!

But there she was, wearing her peach meringue, a flowery crown and a golden heart locket, with this dreamy little Mona Lisa smile on her face. (Later we found out that the smile was because she'd just thought up this wicked bridesmaid-survival strategy, which I'll tell you later! But who cares – it worked!)

Suddenly I peeped out of the window and almost screamed my head off.

There was a *real Rolls Royce* parked outside our house! A genuine cream-coloured Rolls Royce, decorated with white ribbons. Mum's wedding was really happening at last!!

"Remember, girls," said Patsy fiercely. "Stay calm."

"Peaches and Cream Squad – go go go!" commanded Jilly.

Amber rolled her eyes. "Mum, perleaze!"

"Please God, don't let us trip up, and

please, please don't let me get hiccups," I heard Lyndz pray under her breath.

"Amen," said Frankie fervently.

Then Patsy opened the door and all this lovely summer sunlight flooded in. This is too perfect, I thought tearfully. Even the weather is just TOO perfect.

We followed my mother down the garden path, solemnly keeping all her precious satin out of the dirt. (Now I understand why they call them trains. Mum's practically went on for EVER.) But it wasn't until we got outside that we saw just *how* special her train actually was.

A few metres above the hem, there was this big embroidered A.

Do you get it? Sure you do, you nutcase!

The A was for Andy!! Is that romantic or WHAT!!!

Oh, you did remember the ceremony wasn't going to be in an actual church, didn't you? We all had to drive out to this fabulous old Tudor house out in the country. Belvoir Manor, it's called.

I got this absolute STORM of butterflies in

my tummy when we drove up and I saw all the crowds of people waiting for us. I didn't recognise my step-dad at first in his morning coat. Honestly, it was so sweet! When Andy saw Mum in her wedding dress, he was totally lost for words!

He'd somehow found time to get a really smart haircut since we'd last seen him, and he really did look incredibly handsome. Plus I just *loved* his waistcoat. It was embroidered in exactly the same roses and hearts as Mum's dress. Dave, the best man, was cracking these stupid jokes about how it was so Andy didn't go home with the wrong bride by mistake. But Amber and I agreed that it made Mum and Andy look like they totally belonged together.

I'd have liked to give my step-dad a hug actually, but my official train-management duties made this impossible. So Andy made do with giving me a huge wink, and I gave him a very dignified bridesmaid's smile!

The ceremony passed in a flash. I know you'll be relieved to hear that absolutely no-one tripped over, and Lyndz *didn't* have an attack of her famous hiccups, thank goodness!

But the star of the show was definitely my little brother. I don't think I mentioned what a terrible time we'd had getting Callum into his page-boy clothes earlier? I was probably trying to forget it!

Mum's idea was for Callum to walk along with the wedding rings carefully balanced on a small velvet cushion. I had serious doubts about this. He's not the most co-ordinated boy in the world, and his shoes had seriously slippy soles. He wasn't walking really, so much as *skating* over the carpet.

But somehow, even with total strangers watching him, Callum managed to walk down that long strip of red carpet in his strange new page-boy outfit, plus he hung on to those rings like grim death!

I don't think anyone minded that the tip of his tongue was sticking out the whole time. It was only because he was concentrating so hard. And even our vicar laughed when Callum puffed out his cheeks with relief and said, "So now can we have that cake, Mum?"

And suddenly it was over. Mum and Andy were married. *For real!*

The wedding lunch was held in this big marquee. The food was just amazing. We'd all been loads too nervous to eat a bite of breakfast, so everyone was starving.

Mum and Andy had arranged for us bridesmaids to have a special table of our own. But for the first few minutes we all just stuffed our faces, and now and then one of us would go, "Wow, we actually did it."

But eventually, we were all chatting away at once, like we always do.

"It's so great of you guys to invite me to your big wedding sleepover tonight," Amber said suddenly.

"Well, as we're all going to be staying in Fliss's house," grinned Kenny, "it would be pretty rude to have it without you!"

Rosie looked shocked. "You didn't have to say it like that," she said. "Amber might think you mean it."

But Amber just burst out laughing. In a funny way, I think Kenny teasing her made her feel like she was really one of us.

By this time, all the speeches had started. I don't know why grown-ups insist on having them, do you? Next to school assembly, speeches have to be the most boring invention on this planet.

While they were all going on (and on), everyone at our table carried on talking in whispers. Which is when Kenny shared her secret survival strategy to being a bridesmaid.

"I pretended I was invisible," she said calmly. "You guys didn't realise, but the sixth bridesmaid was totally invisible the whole time."

Well, *honestly* – we all fell about. Can you seriously imagine an INVISIBLE bridesmaid helping to hold up a train? Spooky or what!

But by this time, all those angels who'd been busily protecting Lyndz all morning must have gone off duty. And you know what happens when Lyndz gets the giggles? That's right. That girl just EXPLODED into big-time hiccups.

She'd only just gone back to her normal

colour (i.e. not purple) when everyone in the marquee suddenly went completely wild, all clapping and cheering and laughing.

I looked up in amazement, just in time to see Andy return to his seat beside Mum. For some reason they were both grinning like idiots.

"Wow," breathed Amber. "I don't know what your dad just said, Fliss, but everyone really, REALLY loved him."

And all at once Mum was beside me, hugging all the breath out of me.

"Sorry you had to hear it like that, sweetheart," she babbled. "We'd planned to tell you before we went away on our honeymoon. I don't know what got into Andy, blurting it out in front of everyone like that!"

I struggled up for air. Mum was glowing with excitement.

"So what do you think?" she demanded. "I can't believe I've been worrying myself to death all week, thinking something was wrong. And all the time everything was perfectly normal."

I stared at her. "Mum, I haven't a *clue* what you're on about. What do you mean, *normal*?"

"Normal for twins, of course," she cried. "Isn't it amazing! I had the scan yesterday."

I bet you've never seen six bridesmaids in flowery crowns with their mouths hanging open, have you!

"You're having a BABY!" I breathed.

"Two," Kenny corrected me quickly. "She said twins, dummy!"

Mum's eyes were bright with tears. "I wanted to tell you, Flissy," she said. "But the doctor was worried something was wrong. And you had so much on your plate with the wedding and everything, I couldn't bear you to have any extra worries."

Andy appeared beside her. "So what's the verdict?" he said shyly. "I know we must have acted really weird sometimes this week. Are we forgiven, princess?"

But I just jumped into Andy's arms and buried my head in his shoulder.

"Yes," I said in a muffled voice. "You are both totally *totally* forgiven, but don't you

DARE keep me in the dark like that again, OK."

After that, as you can imagine, all of us partied away like mad. And then it was time for Mum and Andy to go off on their honeymoon.

Sometimes I feel deeply depressed at the end of a party, don't you? But by this time, Mum and Andy's news was sinking in just enough for me to realise this party wasn't like an ENDING. It was the beginning of an amazing new life. And that made me feel incredibly safe and happy somehow. You know what I mean?

All the guests turned out to wave and throw confetti as Andy and Mum made a mad dash for their car. At last they got away and everyone started gradually drifting back to the marquee.

Everyone except me. I stood there by myself, with my long dress fluttering in the breeze, and watched the car disappear down the drive. And I stayed there, watching and watching, until it was a teeny weeny dot in the distance.

And then I went back to the marquee, to do some SERIOUS bopping with the others!

CHAPTER ELEVEN

Phew! That's the big water splash out of the way. Now you can really relax and enjoy the rest of the ride. We're almost home and dry!

There's just a few (very tiny) surprises to go...

Hope you've forgiven me for having that tiny freak-out back there? I mean, how many girls have to cope with getting an official new dad AND find out they're getting two new babies in the family, all on the same day? Not many, is my guess!

It's funny – my mates and I generally think of sleepovers as like, the MAJOR exciting event of our school week or whatever. But after all the excitement of the wedding (AND some!) our actual wedding sleepover felt almost, well – RESTFUL.

Like Lyndz said, you'd think that after stuffing ourselves with all that gorgeous wedding food, we'd be totally full to bursting, wouldn't you? But luckily, by the time everyone had stopped watching videos, we were all feeling nicely peckish again! Which was just as well, because when we finally went up to bed, it turned out everyone had brought LOADS of goodies.

In honour of our special guest, we'd decided to give the sleepover feast an American theme! After Jilly and Patsy had been in to say goodnight, we waited till they'd gone back downstairs, then we turned on our torches and shared out our American loot.

Want to know what we had?

We had real American jelly beans – both kinds. The sweet kind and the really sour ones which make your eyes water. They actually make Lyndz shudder all over, but she says they're so delicious that it's worth it!

We also had some real melt-in-your-mouth chocolate brownies. Good old Frankie brought them. She said she just *had* to make it up to me for my horrendous cabbage soup experience! Plus, we had a HUGE family pack of marshmallows. I truly don't understand how something that is basically just a mouthful of fluff can have so many wicked calories, do you? Oh, yes, and we had Oreo cookies. Everyone else raved about them. Personally I didn't think they were that special.

But the Sleepover Club's unanimous favourite were these totally HEAVENLY sweets that Amber provided. They're called Hershey's Chocolate Kisses, would you believe? Kenny joked that it was the first time in her whole life that she'd seen the point of anyone giving you kisses!

Then it was time for everyone to write in their sleepover diaries. Amber didn't own one, obviously, so I said she could write a few lines in mine. This is what she wrote.

147

When I get back home, I'm going to invite all my friends to a sleepover at my house, first chance I get! I have had the most fabulous time here. Plus I haven't laughed so much since Lauren McGravy slid down our stairs on a tea tray, sneezing nonstop!!

"Tell us what you put!" everyone pleaded.

So Amber read it out to us in her laid-back Hollywood voice (which sounded even better by torchlight, for some reason). And this time I don't think the others even *noticed* her using the word 'fabulous'!

Of course, then Amber had to explain to the others all about her ex-best buddy Lauren, with the famous Disney sneeze. But she didn't seem quite so sad when she told it this time. Then Amber gave my diary back to me, and I wrote this:

This has definitely been the most amazing twenty-four hours of my life.

Not only have I been a bridesmaid, got a new dad, AND found out I'm getting two new baby sisters or brothers (or maybe one of each!), but I also finally found out what I want to do when I grow up. I have decided to be a fashion designer. Andy's mum promised that when I'm older, she'll teach me how to make really stylish clothes, just like she used to do at that posh French fashion house in London.

I read this out to everyone. Then the others read out all these sweet things they'd written, about what a great time they'd had, being bridesmaids. Then we all totally ran out of steam. The wedding sleepover was over!

You'd think I'd have gone to sleep really quickly, wouldn't you, after the day I'd had? But it's like Mum says. Sometimes it's possible to get TOO tired.

I did almost drift off, but then suddenly I spun off into a serious doom spiral.

For the first time, it really hit me that in a few months my lovely quiet life was going to be disrupted by – shock, horror (*durn durn DURN!*) –

TWIN BABIES!!!

Aaaargh!! What if Mum and Andy's twins

turn out to be rude little boys, I panicked – the kind who go on about bottoms all the time and mess up their big sister's things, and track mud across her nice pink carpet?

Honestly, I lay there worrying for HOURS. Until finally I fell asleep, completely worn out.

And guess what? The sleepover angels must have come back on duty or something, because I had the sweetest, funniest dream. (Don't tell the others though, because it's private.)

In my dream, I walked out into our garden. Suddenly I heard all these soft little cooing sounds drifting over our neighbours the Watson-Wades's hedge, so I peered over to see what was going on.

And there, where grumpy old Mr Watson-Wade always plants his garden peas, were two gorgeous newborn babies, nestling inside a giant pea pod. (For some reason this didn't seem at all weird at the time!)

"You can SO totally tell they're twins," I said to myself in the dream. "They're as alike as two peas in a pod."

Then I realised what I'd said, and woke myself up laughing!

And I felt so ridiculously happy that I tried to stay awake a few minutes longer, to enjoy the joke...

Have you noticed how everything's slowing down now? That's because we've almost reached the end of the sleepover wedding rollercoaster trip. But there's one last thing I've got to tell you.

I expect you noticed that those lucky somethings kind of dropped out of the story? Also that wedding present?

You thought I'd forgotten about them! Well, thanks a BUNCH!!

You didn't seriously imagine that a superstitious girl like me could let her parents drive off into the sunset with all those clouds of bad luck hanging over them? No WAY!

So don't go just yet, OK, because it's time to unveil Patsy's mysterious late-night project at last.

Can you believe that Andy's mum actually came up with a way to combine my four lucky somethings in a totally unique wedding present?

Here's how we did it. With help from Patsy and Amber, I stitched Mum a beautiful little evening bag. And by the time it was finished, my mind was totally at rest. This bag didn't just LOOK good, I knew it had good luck built into every stitch.

We made it from a piece of gorgeous blue satin (something blue *and* something new). Then Patsy kindly donated one of her lovely lace handkerchiefs, so we could edge it in antique lace (something old).

OK, OK, so you can't imagine Andy getting too excited about an evening bag. Plus I've got to admit the "something borrowed" gave me a real headache. But then Amber said she'd lend me her smart new pen so I could write a special message for both my parents, to put inside the bag.

But I had a better idea.

I did borrow the pen, but I didn't use it to write a message, so much as a rather unusual gift voucher.

This is what it said:

The Sleepover Club Bridesmaids

This entitles Nikky and Andy Proudlove to
one whole year of good behaviour from their
children.

With love from
   Fliss and Callum
xxx

32

Sleepover Girls
See Stars

Greetings, earthlings! When Frankie is given a telescope for a late birthday present, the gang get really excited about star-gazing – and Fliss, of course, goes horoscope mad. But what are those strange green lights they see up on Cuddington Hill one night? Could it possibly be... aliens?!

Pack up your sleepover kit and reach for the skies!

33

Sleepover Club Blitz

It's World War II all over again for the gang when they get to experience a whole weekend in an authentic wartime house. No TV, no mod cons and no inside toilet – yikes! Not to mention scratchy knickers and stodgy food... And when an air-raid siren goes off in the middle of the night, there's creepy-crawlies in the air-raid shelter to worry about too!

The past's a blast with the Sleepover Club!

www.fireandwater.com
Visit the book lover's website

(34)

Sleepover Girls in the Ring

Roll up, roll up, the circus is in town! When Ailsa the circus girl comes to Cuddington Primary, the gang are up for some serious fun when they sort out circus lessons. But whose crazy idea was it to juggle jam doughnuts in Fliss's house? The Sleepover Club is in BIG trouble – and things just get worse when they discover that Kenny's monstrous sister Molly is going to have circus lessons too!

Stick on a red nose and cartwheel over!

Order Form

To order direct from the publishers, just make a list of the titles you want and fill in the form below:

Name ....

Address ....

....

....

Send to: Dept 6, HarperCollins Publishers Ltd, Westerhill Road, Bishopbriggs, Glasgow G64 2QT.

Please enclose a cheque or postal order to the value of the cover price, plus:

UK & BFPO: Add £1.00 for the first book, and 25p per copy for each additional book ordered.

Overseas and Eire: Add £2.95 service charge. Books will be sent by surface mail but quotes for airmail despatch will be given on request.

A 24-hour telephone ordering service is available to holders of Visa, MasterCard, Amex or Switch cards on 0141- 772 2281.

Collins
An *Imprint* of HarperCollins*Publishers*